Val had a happy if h
loved the fact that her
most. Mud (her mother) was trying to become a sculptress; Dad just read books and quoted literature the whole
time; and the twins – they lived in a world of their own,
apart from turning up at mealtimes and embarrassing
visitors! Val is not very beautiful or brilliant at school, but
she's very happy and secure with her crazy family.

Or she was – until the day Mud leaves, just walks out,
and they all have to cope on their own. Suddenly everything is very different and Val loses (for a while) faith
in everything and everyone she loved. How the family
comes to terms with its unusual make-up and how Val
finds her own role is a moving but funny story.

Judy Gardiner has been writing all her life. She was the
daughter of a chorus girl and an army officer but was
brought up by her elderly nanny and sisters. She served
in the WRAC during the Second World War, then married and had two children. She has published several
adult novels.

JUDY GARDINER

# Come Back
# Soon

PUFFIN BOOKS

Puffin Books, Penguin Books Ltd, Harmondsworth, Middlesex, England
Viking Penguin Inc., 40 West 23rd Street, New York, New York 10010, U.S.A.
Penguin Books Australia Ltd, Ringwood, Victoria, Australia
Penguin Books Canada Limited, 2801 John Street, Markham, Ontario, Canada L3R 1B4
Penguin Books (N.Z.) Ltd. 182–190 Wairau Road, Auckland 10, New Zealand

First published by Viking Kestrel 1985
Published in Puffin Books 1987

Library of Congress catalog card number: 86-43072

Made and printed in Great Britain by
Hazell Watson & Viney Limited,
Member of the BPCC Group,
Aylesbury, Bucks

# CHAPTER ONE

It all began on the day Mud came in from the garden carrying a large lump of something white. She put it down on the table where her daughter Val was doing geography homework.

'There now – what d'you think of that?'

'What is it?'

'Can't you see?' Mud looked impatient. 'It's a model of Sheepshanks.'

'Oh . . . yes.' Val studied it more closely. 'Fancy that. Did you make it?'

'Yes.'

Val studied it some more. Then becoming aware that she was expected to comment a little more fully, asked: 'What out of?'

'The stuff you fill cracks in walls with. I found a bag of it down in the cellar.'

This was Mud at her most casual, but behind the airy smile and careless wave of the hand, Val sensed that the chunk of white plaster was very important to her. You could certainly see that it was an animal because it had a tail, but in all honesty no one could swear that it was the dead spit of Sheepshanks, the family dog.

'I think it's super,' Val said with increased warmth. 'I swear it's the dead spit of him.'

'You really think so?' Mud beamed, then darted round the table to peer at her creation from another angle. 'I had a bit of trouble with the hind legs but I expect I'll get better as I go along. After all, Rome wasn't built in a day.'

'You mean you're going to make some more things?'

'Oh yes! I want to have a go at a reclining nude, and I'd love to try doing your father's bust –'

'But Father hasn't got a –'

'And just think, Val, if I get good enough I could have it cast in bronze!'

'Have what cast in –'

'Your father's bust, fathead! . . .' And Mud rattled gaily on, with Val (her mind still partly on geography) stumbling along behind.

'It's all a question of how keen you are. You can achieve anything if you really want to!'

'You'll certainly need a lot of keenness to get good at sculpture.'

'You mean, you don't think I'll ever . . . ?' Abruptly deflated, Mud turned away. Her mouth drooped, her shoulders sagged. She stood picking crumbs of white plaster from the front of her sweater. 'But I've just got to do something to express myself – to have something of my own. Honestly, life's so boring, sometimes. So rottenly predictable . . .'

Not from where I'm sitting it isn't, thought Val. I can't ever predict anything. What marks I'll get in the mid-term tests, whether I'm good enough for the

6

swimming team, or even if Alice'll be speaking to me tomorrow. She hasn't spoken to me for three days now . . . I'd give anything to be the one who makes things happen, instead of just having them happen to me – unpredictably.

Aloud, she said: 'What's for supper?'

'Ham,' said Mud. And left the room.

Well, that's something, Val told herself. Pen in hand, she sat contemplating the model of Sheepshanks and thinking about food.

Because of her mother's mercurial temperament, even that was unpredictable; sometimes they would all be vegetarian because Mud had joined an animal rights campaign; other times they were fed on kidney beans and alfalfa because Mud had read an article about Harmony Beginning in the Stomach, and there had been a short and disastrous raw fish period ('It has been scientifically proved that the Eskimo are the healthiest race on earth . . .'), which had given them all worms.

Her nickname, incidentally, derived from the thick brown liquid purchased at the health food store which was supposed to keep every nutritional disaster permanently at bay, but which tasted (so Father said) like the bed of a badly polluted river.

'You mean it's like mud?'

'Yes,' said Father. Then, because he was a very kind man at heart, added: 'But I daresay even mud can taste quite nice once you've grown accustomed to it.'

During the recent no-fat-no-stodge régime Val had spent a lot of time wangling invitations home to supper with other girls, and on invitationless days spending her pocket money in the hamburger bar opposite the bus station on the way home from school. But for the last few days the family diet had been remarkably like other people's; cornflakes and toast for breakfast, and things like Welsh rarebit or baked beans for the evening meal. It occurred to Val that the longer Mud's restless energy could be diverted from the Importance of Diet into the Art of Sculpture, the longer they might all stand a chance of eating lovely ordinary unhealthy food like everyone else.

'Mud,' she called through the open door, 'I think a bust of Father would be *great* . . .'

There was no answer. With a sigh Val carefully removed the model of Sheepshanks from the top of the atlas, opened it at page 42 and began to search for the source of the Danube.

There were six members of the Hope family, although the elder girl didn't really count as she had left home ('Flounced out in a high-flown huff,' as Father put it). As well as her and Val there were also twin boys who would be starting school in September, then there was Mud, and of course Father.

And if Mud was full of warmth and sunshine and sudden crazy theories and enthusiasms, Father was quiet and gentle and given to fits of extreme absent-mindedness. But it was the absent-mindedness of a scholar, not a scatterbrain, for he was Head of the English Department at the College of Further Education. His great love was for words. The elder Hope girl had been christened Theodosia, which came

8

from the Greek and meant Gift of God, while Val was short for Valeria, which meant a Female Roman Gentile, although her best friend Alice had once said that it sounded more like a skin disease.

As for the twins, they were Bertram and Bardolph respectively, but in their case it didn't matter because they lived deep and mysterious lives of their own, which meant that they were generally someone else anyway. Just now Bertie was an imaginary person called Mr Halleluja, while Bardo was President Polly.

'Polly, as in Polly Parrot?' Mud asked helpfully.

'No,' said Bardo. 'As in Polly Eurathane.'

Like Father, the twins seemed to have been born with a love of words which had largely escaped Val. She was never too sure of them, and she didn't particularly enjoy studying them or pondering their origins. Her heart always sank whenever they had to play word-games, and she particularly hated Scrabble.

Halfway through the splodgy glory of ham and eggs and tomato sauce on that particular evening, she remembered Mud's new interest. And the importance of encouraging it.

'Has anyone seen Mud's wonderful model of Sheepshanks?'

Apparently no one had.

'It's just like him. I think it's great. Mud, can I show them?'

'Later,' Mud said. 'And then only if you *must*.'

But after cramming her mouth with another bit of ham topped by delicious floppy fried egg, Val left the table and returned carrying the lump of white plaster. Reverently she set it down between the cruet and the butter dish.

'There. What did I tell you?'

The twins surveyed it solemnly. Father reached for another slice of bread, mopped his tomato sauce with it, then said: 'Sheepshanks, did you say?'

'Yes,' said Mud in a little muffled voice.

'And you made it?'

'Yes.'

'When?'

'It's taken me nearly a week.'

'What made you do it?' Despite his gentleness, Father was beginning to sound more and more like a heavyweight schoolteacher. Val's heart began to thump in sympathy with his victim.

'I don't know. I – I just wanted to . . .' Not the usual self-confident Mud, this. More like a nervous little girl caught out in something naughty. 'I suppose I just wanted to see if I could do it.'

'Ah.' Still chewing, Father gazed at the model of Sheepshanks. At the dirty smudges on the plaster, at the rough curves and sudden lumpy bits that were meant to be like head and body and legs and tail.

'Its eyes aren't right,' Bardo said.

'I know. I tried lots of times, but . . .'

'Shut up, Bardo,' Val said. 'Sheepshanks' eyes often look like that when he's tired.'

'And his front paws don't match.'

'They're not meant to. I mean, the left one's sup-posed to be tucked up behind the right one.'

'He'd fall over if he stood up.'

10

'For goodness' sake stop carping, you rotten little know-all!'

'I'm not carping,' Bardo said with great dignity. 'I'm merely stating a fact. All animals have paws that match, and his don't, and kindly stop calling me Bardo. My name's Polly.'

'As a model of Sheepshanks, or indeed of any animal,' Father said, laying aside his knife and fork, 'I have come to the conclusion that in the eyes of a layman at least, it is . . .' They all waited, particularly Val and Mud. 'I have to say that I think it's really quite exceptionally good. It has vigour. And life. And a sense of purpose.'

Beneath her own sense of relief, Val heard Mud give a long sigh of gratification. 'You really think so, Paul?'

'Yes. I think you ought to join a class and receive expert tuition.'

'Oh, I'd love that!' Mud's eyes shone. 'But I don't know of –'

'I understand there's a sculpture class being held in the old Technical College,' Father said. 'So you'd better enrol.'

'Well, if you really think . . .'

'I *do* really think.' He sat back and gazed thoughtfully at his empty plate. 'By the way, is there any more ham?'

'No,' said Mud, springing up. 'But it wouldn't take a minute to grill some –'

Catching Father's eye Val realized that he also considered it a good thing to divert Mud's attention from the Importance of Diet into other, less personal

11

channels. She smiled at him, and imagined that she caught the ghost of a wink.

But all he said was: 'Has anyone ever considered what a strange word *mushroom* is?'

'They're nice fried,' said the twin who was President Polly. 'Can we have some?'

'Of course we can,' Mud called from over by the stove. 'We'll buy them tomorrow.'

Val's best friend Alice had pale straight hair and glasses, and nearly always came top in exams. On afternoons when Val wasn't sneaking off to the hamburger bar they generally walked to the bus stop together. Alice and her parents lived in a small expensive flat four stops on from the Hopes' large ramshackle house.

Occasionally Val would wonder how it was that Alice had ever come to be her best friend, because they argued a lot, hardly ever liked the same things, and spent quite a lot of time Not Speaking. At least, it was generally Alice who wasn't, because of some tactless joke or ill-judged remark on the part of Val, and if her apology was not accepted (and it never was, straightaway), Val wouldn't Speak either. After all, there wasn't much point in conversing with herself.

But when they *were* Speaking, Alice seemed to do most of it while Val listened, for Alice knew a lot. Not just about school subjects but about other things as well. Things like politics and the Royal Family and what teachers did during the holidays. She had been the first to know that Mr Nettleton (Chemistry) had been to a disco with Miss Babcock (Physical Education), and that Mrs Royalton (the Head) had spent three days in hospital having her veins done. She also knew that Val's sister Theodosia was a punk, although Val hadn't told her.

But there was a nice side to her as well. She never minded giving Val the answers in maths and French homework, and once gave her a little gold locket when she (Val) trapped her finger in the classroom door and the nail came off. In due course the gold came off the locket too, and Alice admitted that it had come out of a Christmas cracker, but all the same it had been very generous of her.

'My mother's just made a great model of our dog in plaster and she's going to study sculpture.'

'Oh?'

'My mother's going to, not the dog.' Suddenly remembering that they hadn't been Speaking, Val attempted a joke.

'Hmm.'

'In fact she enrolled last night.'

'In the middle of term?' Alice had to start Speaking in order to criticize. 'What a funny idea.'

'The tutor said she was so good that it was a pity to waste time.'

'Hmm,' said Alice. Then added: 'My mother got a degree in home economics when I was only two. That's really something to be proud of.'

'Oh, I dunno.' Val felt obliged to differ. 'Learning things like the price of flour is nowhere near as difficult as expressing yourself in terms of Art.'

'Do you want to come home to supper again?'

Alice said when they were approaching the bus stop. 'You haven't asked for over a week.'

'No, it's all right, thanks.' With Hope family meals still highly satisfactory (fish and chips from the takeaway, sausages and baked beans and lots of cake and biscuits) there was no longer any need. 'In fact,' Val said, 'why don't you come home to supper with us, for a change?'

'I'd have to let my parents know first,' Alice said primly.

'Ring them from our place. Come on, here's the bus . . .'

They got on, and Alice gave Val the answers to the maths homework before they got off at the stop nearest the Hopes' house.

By now, three more Works of Art had been added to the model of Sheepshanks. One was a head and shoulders, supposedly of Father but the nose was wrong; there was another one of a bird, and the largest was an unidentifiable lump with a kind of stalk rising from the middle.

'What's that one?' Alice asked, upon being introduced to it.

'Oh, that's her Revival of Life. It's an abstract.'

'Hmm,' said Alice. She always said that when she thought things but preferred not to put them into words.

In the big old kitchen the normal untidiness had been increased by a large structure on the floor over by the fridge. It proved to be a double blanket spread tentwise over the backs of four chairs, and Val and Alice stood watching the bulges in it appear and disappear as whoever was inside shifted position. A faint glow seemed to shine through it, and their ears caught the low murmur of voices, the subdued clink of metal on china.

'Sounds as if someone's cooking in there,' Alice whispered.

Then the blanket bulged with increased violence, the chairs rocked, and out burst Sheepshanks with his front legs inserted through the arms of someone's white shirt. It was buttoned down his back, and when he saw Val he floundered over to her, showing all his teeth in a grin of embarrassed delight. A twin with a bicycle torch attached to his forehead emerged behind him.

'Bardo, what on earth are you doing?'

'There is no further cause for alarm,' Bardo said. 'We have removed the appendix and the patient is recovering.'

Bertie shuffled out on all fours, dragging a pudding basin and two spoons. 'Hello,' he said. 'I'm Dr Webb.'

'I though you were Mr Halleluja.'

'So I am. There's no harm in being two people at once.'

Val began to unbutton Sheepshanks' improvised theatre gown, and recognized the shirt as her own. But before she could remove it the front door banged and Sheepshanks skidded away to welcome whoever had arrived.

Father came in, looked round at the chaos and said mildly: 'Are we moving house?'

'This is Alice,' Val said. 'She's come to supper.'

15

'What a good idea. Where's Mud?'

'I don't know. Around, I expect.'

'Please may I telephone my parents?' Alice asked. 'They don't know where I am.'

'No one in this house ever seems to know where they are,' Father said. 'But please, help yourself, Angela – the phone's over there –'

'Alice,' Alice said politely. 'I'm Alice Fuller, Mr Hope.'

The twins stood regarding her in silence, while Father stood regarding the twins.

'Bardo, why are you wearing a miner's lamp?'

'It's not a miner's lamp,' Bardo said. 'It's a surgeon's.' He began to detach it from his forehead.

'What sort of minors have special lamps?' Val asked. 'I mean, we don't.'

'The sort that go underground, of course,' said Bertie.

'I don't know any that –'

'Not minors meaning people under age,' Alice said, as if dealing with an idiot. 'Miners meaning men who dig for coal.'

'Well, how was I supposed to know . . .' Val went pink.

'A miner's lamp is called a Davy lamp,' Father explained to the twins. 'And it was so called after its inventor, a chap called Sir Humphry Davy, and I believe that it first came into use as early as 1816 or thereabouts.'

'Your little *brothers* are very bright, aren't they?' Alice said to Val as she passed her to reach the phone. She dialled her home number, then the front

16

door banged again and they heard Mud's voice talking gaily to someone.

She came into the kitchen, her bright red curls bouncing and her eyes shining.

'This is Mr Bridge, who's going to teach me sculpture,' she said. 'He's my tutor, and he's agreed to come to supper. We met in the supermarket, by the way.' She dumped her shopping bag on a chair.

'We've never had a tutor for supper before,' commented Bertie.

'Under your dear mother's influence we've tried most things, but so far, I agree, we've never sampled an academic,' Father said. 'Bertie, one has a guest *to* supper, not *for*.'

The man called Bridge came further into the room and greeted them all with a genial wave of the hand. He was youngish – about the same age as Mud, which meant younger than Father – and he had wavy fair hair and very blue eyes. He perched himself on the edge of the table and said how nice it was to meet them all.

He caught sight of Bertie, who was now wearing the pudding basin on his head. 'Hello, what's your name?'

'Halleluja.'

'Amen to that!'

'And this is President Polly. He's my brother.'

'You're very alike, aren't you?'

'That's because we're identical twins,' Bardo explained. 'Which, incidentally, are not all that easy to come by.'

'Yes, Mummy,' Alice was saying on the phone.

17

'Yes, Mummy dear, I do promise I'll be home before nine-thirty . . . yes, Mummy dear, I *know* you do . . .'

'Do what?' asked Val.

'Worry,' replied Alice, replacing the receiver. 'My mother worries dreadfully about me.'

She looked so neat and smug standing there in the large, dishevelled kitchen that it made Val want to giggle. And when Sheepshanks bounded in still wearing his theatre gown and the man called Bridge asked whether he was a dog or a runaway choirboy, the giggles rose like bubbles in a glass of lemonade.

She suddenly felt that she loved her family very much, and was very glad that they were not like Alice's small orderly world, with dear Mummy and Daddy so careful and solemn and prone to worry. She loved them because they were all so different and so vivid, and she didn't mind a bit about them all being brighter at things than she was. She didn't even mind making a fool of herself over miners and minors.

And on that particular evening Mud was the brightest and most vivid of them all. Laughing and twinkling, she showed her new Works of Art to Mr Bridge (by now, everyone was calling him Bill), then in between restoring the kitchen to order and releasing Sheepshanks from his theatre gown she cooked a spaghetti bolognaise, found a bottle of wine, laid the table, told a funny joke, then changed her dress and brushed her hair before calling that supper was ready.

'Is your mother always like this?' Alice asked in an undertone.

'Oh yes, always,' Val said proudly. 'She can always do six things at once and she never gets cross.'

Loyalty made Alice say that her mother could do more than six, except when she was worried.

Before they began on the spaghetti bolognaise (all squelchy with tomato and crusty with cheese), Bill Bridge raised his glass of wine, smiled round at everyone and said: 'I suggest we drink a toast to our future sculptress!' So everyone raised their glasses, whether they contained wine or coke, and shouted: 'Here's to Mud!' With the exception of Alice, who called her Mrs Hope.

It was all marvellous family fun, and not long after Val was to look back on that evening as the last happy one she could remember.

# CHAPTER TWO

Spring term was now well advanced, the days were lengthening, and early in March Val discovered that she had been picked for the school swimming team.

She was very, very pleased, and couldn't help boasting a bit, particularly to Alice. For Alice was rotten at most sports, and carefully avoided swimming because she couldn't endure having water in her ears.

'I'm down for the junior back crawl and I'm in the relay and I'm having extra coaching in diving! . . .'

'So's Marilyn Phillips. She's really good –'

'She can't do a racing dive –'

'Hers is as good as yours any day –'

'Come off it, Ali, she doesn't keep her feet together . . .'

Val boasted at home as well, but it didn't seem to make a lot of impact there either. Father just nodded vaguely, Mud said: *'Marvellous* – have you seen the nail scissors anywhere? . . .' And when she told the twins they merely came out of their private world long enough to ask what she would feel like if she drowned.

But the pride and the happiness persisted, and

almost every afternoon after school she went across the playing fields to the sports centre and spent half an hour in the swimming pool. In between practising diving and back crawl it was very pleasant to float spreadeagled in the calm water and dream of the triumphs to come.

The only other person who frequented the pool at that hour was a boy of about her own age. She didn't know his name, although she had seen him at school, and guessed that he too had been picked for the team. To begin with they ignored one another, and as if by unspoken agreement kept to their own sides of the pool.

But one day when Val broke surface after a dive from the centre springboard, the boy said: 'That was good. One of your best, so far.'

She shook the water from her eyes and swam over to the side. He was standing there with his wet hair slicked back and his arms folded, looking down at her.

'You really think so?' She clung to the bar that ran round the side of the pool. 'Hope I'll be okay by July.'

'You in the team?'

'Yes. You too?'

'Uh-huh.'

Abruptly he dived in and swam away from her. She watched his arms cutting through the water, the froth of greeny-blue spray kicked up by his beating heels. He swam back.

'What's your name?'

'Rob Lacey. What's yours?'

'Val Hope. I've seen you in assembly.'

They didn't say much more, and left the pool separately, but it felt like the beginning of a friendship.

He was there again on the following day. 'What's the team got you down for?'

'Back crawl and diving. And I'm in the relay.'

'So am I.'

'That's nice . . .'

'Come on, I'll race you – one, two, three – *go!* –'

They went, side by side down the length of the pool with the water churning, and Mr Cook, the swimming coach, watched through the window of his little office.

Rob won, but only by an arm's length. They hooked their feet under the bar and lay back on the water laughing and panting. Then Mr Cook came out and told Rob that he wasn't keeping his elbows up properly. He demonstrated the armstroke, Rob copied, and Val said he looked like a chicken flapping its wings. He pushed her under the water, she dragged him down with her and they both disappeared in a boiling fountain of spray.

Mr Cook walked away with a tolerant smile, and coming out of the dressing rooms with damp hair and pink-rimmed eyes Rob broke a Mars bar in two and gave half to Val. It really did seem like the beginning of a friendship, but for some reason she didn't feel like telling anyone about it. Certainly not Alice.

*

And Mud wasn't telling much either; not about her sculpture anyhow.

She had been attending Bill Bridge's classes for quite a while now, but she didn't bring any Works of Art home. She didn't bring Bill Bridge home again either, which rather pleased Val. Although he was friendly and nice-looking, there was something about him she didn't greatly care for.

One evening the question of summer holidays came up. Generally it was Mud who started the ball rolling soon after Christmas ('Where shall we go? Let's do something crazy – hire a minibus and go to India . . . or what about Greenland? I believe it's quite pretty in the summer . . .'). They never got to places like that, of course, but they had a lot of fun talking about them, and afterwards were quite content to settle for renting a cottage in Wales or Devonshire.

But this year it was Val who said: 'We had a programme at school about Venice sinking. It's going down a terrific number of feet every year and soon it'll be completely under water. Can we go and see it before it is?'

No one said anything.

'Couldn't we go for our summer holiday? If we went tourist and travelled at night and didn't eat much, perhaps it wouldn't cost a lot.'

But Father went on reading his book, and behind the sofa the twins went on quietly talking to one another in the private language they had recently invented, while Mud just went on drumming her fingers and staring at them as if they belonged to someone else.

'I mean,' Val was becoming discouraged, 'we generally go *somewhere*, and we haven't planned anything yet, have we?'

Then Mud said an amazing thing: 'I don't particularly want to go on holiday anywhere.'

It even made Father look up. Marking his place in the book with his finger, he said: 'Not anywhere? Not even *Barmouth*?'

'Least of all,' said Mud, 'do I feel like going to Barmouth.'

'But we must go somewhere,' Val said. 'I mean, we always do, don't we?'

'So what alternative do you suggest?' Father was looking across at Mud with increased attention.

She shrugged. 'I've already told you, I don't want to go on holiday at all.'

'Why not?'

'Because it's all too much – oh, I don't know – too much time and energy to spend on something that's become boringly routine.'

'Ouch,' Father closed his book and laid it aside. 'I didn't realize that family holidays had become a source of tedium, Penny.'

'Our holidays are always super!' Val protested. 'We couldn't be without them –'

'In that case,' Mud looked up for the first time, 'what's to stop you going without me?'

No one said anything. Even the twins stopped murmuring behind the sofa.

'Go without you?' Val began.

'Quiet, Val,' Father said. Then added: 'Is that what you want, my dear?'

'Yes. No. Oh, I don't know . . .' Looking suddenly tired and unhappy, Mud got up from the chair and walked out.

Glancing unobtrusively at her father Val badly wanted to say something. In the end she said: 'Shall I go and make us some coffee?'

'That would be nice,' he said. 'Take a cup to your mother as well.'

He reached for his book and began to read, and Val went out to the kitchen thinking that she had never heard him refer to Mud as 'your mother' in that way before. It sounded strange and sad and rather ominous.

Nothing more was said about the holiday, but a few nights later Val heard the sound of voices coming from her parents' bedroom. The door was slightly open, and although they were speaking in low voices she could hear almost every word.

'Well, then, go without me,' Mud was saying. 'Surely you're capable of taking the children on holiday without my help?'

'Supposing we don't want to go without you?'

'Oh, don't be ridiculous, Paul! Two weeks apart would probably do a world of good –'

'Do who or what a world of good?'

'Everything. Our relationship, for one thing.'

'I wasn't aware,' Father said, 'that there was anything wrong with our relationship.'

'I'm not saying there is, but . . .'

Aware that it was rotten to eavesdrop, Val crept

a bit closer. Her heart was beating unpleasantly fast.

'But what, Penny?'

'I've got other plans.'

'So let's hear them.'

There was a long pause. 'I just want to be on my own,' Mud's voice said finally. 'I want to be on my own to think.'

'What about?'

'It doesn't concern you.'

'I've an uneasy feeling that it does,' Father said, and hearing his footsteps approaching the door, Val fled silently into her own room.

She wondered what was wrong with them. They had never behaved like this before – at least, she didn't think so . . . Feeling puzzled and rather aggrieved she sat down on the side of the bed with her hands between her knees.

After a few minutes Bertie came in wearing Sheepshanks' collar and lead tied round his waist. He laid a carefully folded piece of paper on her lap then stood back and saluted.

'What's this?'

'It's from the President. War's been declared.'

'Oh? Who by?'

'Us,' said Bertie. 'Against Them.'

Plucking at the metal studs in Sheepshanks' collar he inserted them in an imaginary gun, squinted along its barrel and fired a brisk salvo at the ceiling. He fell in a heap on the bedside rug, writhed briefly and then lay still.

'They've shot you!'

'Oh no, that was me shooting one of Them.'

'Oh, I see,' Val said. Then: 'Bertie, what would you say if we didn't go on holiday this year?'

Bertie scrambled to his feet and stared at her, but there was nothing in his stare to suggest concern at the idea of being holidayless.

'If you don't read the President's letter he'll have you put in prison,' he said, and making a noise like machine-gun fire, turned on his heel and marched out.

Idly Val unfolded the piece of paper. It was covered in squiggles interspersed with various letters of the alphabet, some of them written back to front, and it was funny to think what a lot of things the twins knew before they'd even learned to read or write. She hoped they wouldn't turn into awful little swots when they went to school in September.

Reaching for the pen on her bedside table she squiggled a reply on the back, shaped it into a paper dart and aimed it down the stairs towards the sound of battle.

'Janice Brewer's mother's run off with another man,' Alice said during break. They were sitting on the grass outside the science block, eating biscuits and inhaling the scent of late wallflowers. Bees buzzed and the sun was warm.

'She wants to go on living with her father, but he goes abroad a lot, so she can't. She's got to go and live with her auntie.'

'Janice Brewer's stuck up,' Val said.

'She used to be, but she isn't now, poor thing. She's just miserable.'

Val crunched another biscuit without saying anything.

'I don't think people's parents ought to do things like that,' Alice said. 'Mummy and Daddy say it's because it's fashionable to be self-centred these days, but when people have children they've no right to be. They should consider *them*.'

'Yes,' Val said thoughtfully. 'I suppose they should.'

'But of course dozens of people get divorced –'

'Oh, not *dozens!*'

'Yes, they do. It said in our paper the other day that one out of every three marriages is doomed to failure from the start, and that by the time it's our generation's turn it'll be even worse.'

'Well, it doesn't bother me, because I'm not going to get married anyway.'

'Why not?'

'I don't suppose anyone'd have me.'

Alice removed her glasses, polished them on her skirt, and then settled them back on her nose. She then turned her attention to Val, and sat looking at her critically. 'Oh, I don't know. You're a bit untidy, but not all that bad-looking.'

'And I'm not very bright at things. Except swimming.'

'No, that's true,' Alice agreed. 'Although Mummy says that you don't have to be intellectual to make

28

a good wife and mother. You just need patience and ordinary common sense and the ability to go on and on.'

'Mmm.' Val sat thinking about Mud, who never had any patience. She couldn't even plant anything without digging it up two days later to see how it was getting on.

'But the trouble with Janice Brewer's mother,' Alice went on, 'is that she's just simply run away. Janice says the man's name is Harry and he's in the haulage business.'

'My mother hasn't got a lot of patience and isn't keen on just going on and on, but she's very good at being married,' Val said.

'As for my parents, they never quarrel,' Alice said with a smirk. 'Our friends all say they've never seen a family as happy as ours.'

'Don't they even get a bit fed up sometimes?' It was suddenly important to know about other people's parents; to compare notes and see how Mud and Father measured up.

'No, never,' Alice affirmed. 'They're always loving and patient and good-tempered and they never change. You must have noticed – all the times you've been to supper.'

Her smirk began to get on Val's nerves. Grabbing the last biscuit she bit it in half with a loud snap.

'When I say my mother hasn't got a lot of patience, I don't mean with *us*. Whatever *we* do she never gets cross, in fact I heard her saying to my father the other night that she didn't know what she'd do if

29

she hadn't got us. It's all because of us that she's inspired to make Works of Art and try out new ideas – we all stimulate her, she said.'

'You've got crumbs all down your front,' Alice said coldly.

The bell sounded just then, so there was no time to say more. They walked across the grass to the junior school and Val remembered that the next lesson was history.

'I've forgotten who it was the king invited to the Field of the Cloth of Gold.'

'Henry the Fifth of France,' said Alice. 'Don't you know *anything*?'

'Oh, stop being so clever. Trouble with you is you just know everything! . . .'

They walked on, stiff with crossness, and the new spell of Not Speaking promised to be a long one.

During the days that followed, Val somehow couldn't get the thought of Janice Brewer's mother out of her mind. She had seen her once or twice at school functions wearing short tight skirts and wafting strong perfume, and the thought of her running away with someone was awful. In some odd way it was embarrassing, and rotten for Janice, even if she was stuck up.

At home, Mud still wasn't saying much, and although she was now going to art classes two nights a week she still wasn't bringing any new Works of Art home for them to see. If Val asked how she was getting on she would just give a quick shrug and say: 'Oh, so-so,' which didn't mean anything, and once Val said: 'Perhaps you don't want me to ask about your sculpture, but I wouldn't mind you asking about my swimming.'

'Oh yes, how is it?'

'I did a hundred metres back crawl in three minutes two seconds.'

'That sounds very quick!' Mud smiled at her, and just for a moment the light came back into her eyes.

'You will be coming to the gala, won't you? It's on July the eighteenth.'

'Yes, of course I will,' Mud said. Then added sharply: 'Why do you ask?'

'Oh, I dunno,' Val mumbled. 'I just thought you might be – well, busy . . .'

'Hmm,' said Mud. And it was like Alice at her most disparaging.

Val was still thinking about Janice's mother three days later when on the way home from school someone seized her by the elbow and said: 'Well, well – how's tricks?'

It was Bill Bridge, Mud's tutor, sauntering along with a string bag full of groceries. He looked very handsome in Levis and an open-necked check shirt.

'Oh, hello.' Val removed her elbow from his grasp as politely as possible. Not knowing what else to say, she stood looking down at his shopping. A bottle of sherry was nestled between a lettuce and a long French loaf.

'Got someone nice coming to supper tonight,' he said. 'Someone worth making a special effort for.'

'Oh?' She still didn't know what else to say. His

eyes were very blue and his teeth were very white and she still didn't like him.

'Been swimming, have you?' He swung into step beside her, and she became conscious of her half-dried hair and the bit of striped towel poking out of the holdall she used for a satchel.

'Yes. I go most afternoons after school.'

'I loved swimming when I was your age. I was in the school team.'

'Were you?'

If it had been anyone else but Bill Bridge she would have enjoyed talking about it; would have been eager to tell about the hundred metres back crawl, and how the instructor had said that her racing dive was coming on well – in a way she was quite hungry to talk to someone about swimming who understood about it and was keen – but somehow she couldn't with him.

'Does your mother like swimming?'

'Not very much. She says it's always too cold.'

'We'll have to try and warm her up then, won't we?' Bill Bridge said, and the laughter in his voice made Val's cheeks turn bright pink.

'I like your mother,' he said, and took her elbow again as they crossed the road. 'She's very clever, and she's also great fun.'

'Yes, I know.' For the second time Val wrenched her elbow away. 'My father thinks so, too.'

She stalked off without saying goodbye, and trundling home on the bus told herself that she wouldn't have got upset if it hadn't been for Janice's mother.

It was very quiet in the house. The kitchen was

deserted, and when she hung her swimming things out to dry she saw the twins at the bottom of the garden digging a hole. She waved, but they looked at her without any hint of recognition, because she wasn't part of their game.

So she went back to the kitchen and poured herself a glass of milk before settling down at the table with her homework. They had to do an essay on the ceremony of Trooping the Colour, which they had been told to watch on TV, and she had written nearly two pages when she became vaguely aware of footsteps behind her chair and of someone reading over her shoulder.

'Fixed *bayonets*,' Father said. 'Not bear nets.'

'I'm sure it's bear nets. Positive . . .'

'Then tell me, why should they need nets for bears in the middle of London?'

'I don't know,' Val looked harassed. 'But they wear bearskins on their heads, don't they?'

Father smiled and patted her shoulder. 'At least you're a fairly logical person,' he said. 'Has anyone made any tea?'

He filled the kettle and switched it on. Val sat with her pen poised, ready to strike out 'bear nets' and substitute 'bayonets', then hesitated. It seemed a pity to spoil a nice neat page.

'I understand that the word bayonet is derived from the French town of Bayonne, where they were first made,' Father said, lightly dropping a tea-bag into a mug. 'On the other hand, it may well derive from the Old French word *bayon*, meaning arrow.'

'Oh. I see.'

'Horrible things, bayonets.' He shuddered.

'Worse than the Bomb?'

'Much less efficient, but much more personal. Let's change the subject.'

The kettle began to sing and Val sat rattling her pen against her front teeth. 'It's all over our school that Janice Brewer's mother's run off with another man.'

'Good heavens,' Father murmured. 'Does he mind?'

'Who – the man?'

'No, Janice Brewer's father.'

'Oh, I don't know. I never thought to ask. But it's pretty awful for poor old Janice, even though she is stuck up –'

'Is that the girl who came here to supper that time?'

'No, that was Alice. She's stuck up too, but in a different sort of way.'

'Stuck . . . up . . .' Father repeated quietly and despairingly to himself, and Val waited with resignation to be told how the expression originated, from what language, and so on. But he poured the boiling water on to his teabag in silence, swished it round a few times and then fished it out with the aid of Val's ruler.

'When I was a little boy I used to pretend that I was the captain of one of the old tea-clippers, those marvellous fast sailing ships that used to skim down through the Indian Ocean, delicate as butterflies, and then battle their way round the Cape of Good Hope

34

in dreadful storms . . . I was often shipwrecked, but I never drowned.'

'You were just like the twins!' Val said in wonderment. 'They're always pretending to be someone else.'

Adding milk and sugar to the mug, Father seated himself. He was sitting opposite Val, and he looked at her with equal wonderment. 'You've never gone in for that, have you? Pretending to be someone else, I mean.'

'No, not really. I seem to have enough trouble just being me. Perhaps it's because I'm not as bright as the rest of you.'

'What *do* you like doing?' Although he was looking at her very kindly, she couldn't help thinking how nice it would be if he said that she *was* bright. Just as bright as anyone else. But he didn't.

'I like swimming,' Val said. 'I'm in the school team and I did a hundred metres back crawl in –'

But just at that moment Mud came in, Sheepshanks bounding at her side. Father went through the process of making another mug of tea and then handed it to her.

'Thanks, Paul.'

'Val and I were talking about what we like doing. Her favourite thing's swimming, and she's in the school team.'

'Yes, I know,' Mud said. 'Has anyone seen the twins?'

'They're in the garden digging a hole,' Val said.

In between taking sips of tea, Mud began rummaging in the freezer. She came up with a large packet of fish in batter, a packet of peas and some individual fruit pies. She heaped them on the table, together with a bag of potatoes.

'You may not believe this, but you're going to cook for yourselves tonight,' she announced. 'It's all quite simple, just follow the instructions on the packets, then peel the potatoes and cook them whichever way you like.'

'Another art class?' Father asked.

'You generally do supper before you go out,' Val said.

'I know I generally do supper before I go out, but this time is different. And no, Paul, I am not going to another art class.'

Mud gave a sudden brilliant smile, and Val noticed then that she had put on her new Indian dress with the silver embroidery. Her red hair was freshly shampooed and she was wearing green eyeshadow. 'No, as a matter of fact I'm going out to supper.'

'What, on your own?' For the first time Father looked frankly amazed.

'Yes. Why not?'

'But who with?'

'Oh, nobody special,' Mud said.

Bending low over her homework Val closed her eyes when she remembered Bill Bridge and his string bag full of shopping and a bottle of sherry.

*Got someone nice coming to supper tonight*, he had said. *Someone worth making a special effort for . . .*

Don't go, Val whispered inside her head. Don't go, or you'll end up like Janice's mother . . .

She opened her eyes in time to see Mud plant a

light kiss on Father's cheek, then turn in a girlish pirouette of flowery Indian cotton and make for the door.

'Don't bother to wait up,' she cried gaily. 'I won't be in until very late!'

# CHAPTER THREE

It was a long while before sleep crept up on Val that night.

She lay in the dark, fidgeting restlessly and trying not to see pictures of Mud and Bill Bridge having supper together; but as soon as she managed to blot them out, their place would be taken by Janice Brewer's mother in her short tight skirt and awful perfume.

Alice was quite right when she said that parents should consider their children and not be self-centred. And it *was* self-centred to go off having supper on their own with someone of the opposite sex. Sex, thought Val; even the word's horrible . . .

Next morning Mud had breakfast in her housecoat. She looked rumpled and sleepy, and when Val asked if she'd had a nice time she just said: 'Yes. Lovely.'

For a moment it felt as if she was going to say something more, but she didn't. And as Val didn't feel like asking for details – and, judging from his expression, neither did Father – no more was said by anyone.

She went swimming that afternoon, but now that the weather was warmer there were more people in the pool, which made it more difficult to practise. It was impossible to swim a complete length without bumping into someone, and when she caught sight of the boy Rob she hauled herself out of the water and sat on the side, next to him.

'I know a better place than this,' he said.

'Oh? Where?'

'Beauchamp Park. There's a big lake there.'

'But it's private, isn't it?'

'I know. But there's never anyone about – I've been swimming there lots of times.'

Val didn't say anything. She just sat with her feet dangling in the water and listening to the other swimmers' shouts and screams echoing against the walls.

'Have you got a bike?' Rob asked. 'It's the only way to get there.'

She said she had, and agreed to cycle there with him on the following afternoon.

'But supposing we get caught?'

'They can't charge us with trespassing,' Rob said, 'unless they can prove that we've damaged things.' Like Alice, he seemed to know a lot.

It was a long ride, and although she wasn't fond of cycling she quite enjoyed it; they didn't talk much, but Rob always rode on the outside and didn't show off by going too fast.

Beauchamp Park was an old mansion set in quiet green countryside outside the city boundary. The County Council was supposed to have bought it when the last owners left, but hadn't done much with it. In the meanwhile it was becoming more and

39

more neglected, and it was quite easy to sneak through one of the crumbled gateways and creep through the overgrown woods.

The lake was set in front of the silent, shuttered old house, and it must have been very beautiful at one time with its stone dolphins and remains of a big fountain in the middle. But there were bulrushes growing in the water now, and after the clear clean blue of the swimming pool it looked discouragingly murky.

'How deep is it?'

'Difficult to say, because if you try to stand up you sink in.'

'Ergh . . .'

'Come on, it's great once you get going.'

There were lots of trees to undress behind, and, as Rob had said, it was great once you got going. The water had a soft, almost silky feel and was surprisingly warm. They swam up and down quietly and rather solemnly, because Beauchamp Park was a quiet and solemn sort of place; if they laughed and shouted they might disturb the ghosts of past owners, Val thought.

'I like it here,' she said as they climbed out. 'Do you think lots of other people swam in it too?'

'Not the Victorians, anyway,' Rob said, draping his towel round his shoulders. 'They were all so funny and prudish – and just think of all the clothes they had to take off before they could start . . .'

For some reason his words reminded her of the word she hated. The word that made her think of Janice Brewer's mother, and of Mud having supper with Bill Bridge. That three-letter word beginning with S.

Without replying she went back behind her tree and began to dry herself in private. She didn't even want Rob to see her drying her hair.

'But I bet they sailed a boat on it,' he called. 'There'd be plenty of room to sail a boat . . . .'

During the ride home she glanced at his profile once or twice. A thick bob of dark hair hanging over a child's snub nose and a boy's firm mouth, and she had to admit that in some ways he was nicer to be with than Alice.

There was a row when she got back.

'Where have you been?' Mud looked furious.

'Swimming. Why?'

'You're over an hour late.'

Val blinked. 'Well, we went to another place. To a lake.'

'Who's *we*?'

Without quite knowing why, Val said: 'Me and another girl.'

Mud made the Alice noise (*Hmm*), then said in a voice that now sounded more weary than angry: 'Didn't it occur to you that we might be worried to death?'

'No,' Val said, genuinely surprised.

'You're as vague as your father. Well, you could at least say you're sorry.'

'I'm sorry.'

'You don't sound it.'

'Well, I am. What's for supper?'

Before Mud could reply, Father came in. 'I can't

find one of my black shoes.' He hovered in the doorway wearing his dark suit.

'Wear your brown ones, then.'

'How can I, with a navy blue suit?'

'Break with tradition,' Mud said pitilessly. 'Your elder daughter wears no shoes at all and paints her face in stripes, your younger daughter goes off swimming in a lake somewhere and comes home an hour late, while your two sons –'

'Whenever our children behave less than perfectly they're always described as mine,' Father said. 'There's a certain amount of give-and-take in parenthood as well as marriage, you know.'

'I've long realized that I take far more than I give when it comes to plain aggro –'

'Yes, dear. Now, about my shoe –'

'I saw it in Sheepshanks' basket this morning,' Val said. 'At least, I think I did –'

A blood-curdling scream drowned her words and Bertie rushed in and hurled himself at Mud. 'I've hurt myself – I've hurt myself!'

'Where? Where have you?' Unrolling him from the folds of her skirt, she examined him rapidly.

'My head! I fell out of the tree when I was hanging him!'

'Oh, my God,' said Father. 'Hanging who?'

'The President – he's really the leader of all of Them, and he –'

'The Pre – d'you mean Bardo? Oh, you stupid little boy, why don't you call people by the same names as everyone else does –' Mud began.

'I think we'd better go and find him –' Father

started towards the door and collided with Bardo, who was just coming in. Bardo fell over.

'He's hurt his head . . . oh dear, oh dear, he's fell down on his head –'

'Fallen, not fell. And what's all this about hanging?' Father hauled him upright. 'What sort of a game d'you call that?'

Without bothering to reply Bardo darted across to Bertie. They put their thin little arms round one another's waists and hugged close, their identical faces pressed together, their identical voices murmuring mysterious comfort and consolation.

'Boys,' Father began, 'I forbid you to play games that involve hanging people –'

'Shut up – shut up – all of you!' Mud shrieked, and clapping her hands over her ears rushed out of the kitchen. They heard her footsteps pounding across the hall.

'Listen,' Father appealed to Val, 'I'm due at a governors' meeting at the college in half an hour and I can't go in one shoe – people will think me eccentric . . .'

'Hang on while I go and look in Sheepshanks' basket.'

Groping through the folds of blanket Val unearthed bones and other private treasures, but no shoe. Eventually they found it under the table in the dining room. Hurriedly Father put it on, smoothed his hair, snatched up his briefcase and departed while the twins trailed reluctantly upstairs towards bath and bed.

It seemed very quiet in the house, then. So quiet

43

that the sudden ring of the doorbell made Val jump violently. She went to answer it.

'Hello, young Val.' It was Bill Bridge, of all people.

'Oh — hello.' She stood holding the door without smiling.

'I've called round to see your mother. Is she at home?'

The awful nerve of the man. She couldn't get over it. 'I don't know,' she said through stiff lips. 'I'll — I'll have to go and see.'

He followed her into the hall, and beneath the friendly smile she sensed that he was anxious. Worried, even. It didn't alter her dislike of him.

'Wait in there,' she said, indicating the empty sitting room, then turned her head at the sound of footsteps running downstairs.

'Oh, Bill . . .' Mud said, and looked for a minute as if she wanted to bolt back upstairs again. She ran her hand through her hair. 'What have you come for?'

'I want to talk to you,' Bill Bridge said. 'I want to know what's wrong.'

'Nothing's wrong . . .'

'In that case, why have you suddenly given me up?' And while Val stood watching he seized Mud's elbow and marched her into the sitting room. He closed the door.

Open-mouthed with shock, Val crept closer. Yes, of course eavesdropping was rotten, but there were times when it was necessary. She put her ear close to the crack and heard Mud saying something in a low monotone.

Then Bill Bridge said: 'But listen, everyone who's serious gets doubts, but they just soldier on. You'd be crazy to give everything up now – surely you can see that?'

Again Mud made a sort of low mumble. Bill Bridge began to protest but Mud's low mumble went on, obviously trying hard to explain something. It was impossible to hear the words, but the tone was sad and dispirited and for a moment Val toyed with the idea of rushing in and saying *Leave my mother alone! She's nothing to do with you!* But she didn't. She just went on crouching there, cold and sick at heart.

'So are you trying to say that I'm not good enough for you?' This was Bill Bridge again.

'Oh no, please don't think that –' Mud's voice rose for a moment, then flopped again.

'Cheer up, Penny, and don't lose confidence. What we're doing now may not look right to you, but take it from me that it *is* . . .'

Val couldn't stand it any longer. Shattered beyond belief she crept away up to her room and stayed there until the twins' loud swishings and splashings in the bathroom began to get on her nerves. She had gone back to the kitchen and was trying hard to concentrate on homework when she heard the front door bang. A few seconds later Mud came in.

Val wanted to say *Has he gone?* but the words wouldn't come.

'He's gone,' Mud said.

Val wanted to ask *For ever?* but managed no more than a strangled croak.

Mud sighed, and then did something she hadn't

45

done for ages. She came up behind Val, linked her arms round her shoulders and kissed the top of her head. It made Val cry, but only quietly.

'Dear old Val,' Mud said, and ruffled her hair.

'It's all going to be all right, isn't it?'

'Yes, love, of course it is,' Mud said. And they held hands, squeezing them and pressing them together as if they could never bear to let go.

The next day was Saturday, and the knowledge that Mud had sent Bill Bridge packing made Val start thinking about the family, and about how important families were when you *did* start thinking about them. And when her thoughts got round to including her sister Theodosia, she decided on the spur of the moment to go and see her.

Theodosia had left home three years ago when she was sixteen, and although Mud and Father had put a sort of comically resigned face on it, Val could remember fragments of scenes and heated discussions, of tears and rages, and even of a hushed-up visit to the juvenile court when Theo was officially regarded as being In Need of Care and Protection. ('So how do you go about protecting someone who doesn't wish to be protected?' Father had demanded. 'Tie her to the leg of the bed?')

But Theo had refused to come home, just as she had refused to go on being educated, and after a couple of perilous periods as mother's help to families who were prepared to Treat Problem Girls with Sympathy, she moved into a large and semi-derelict house inhabited by squatters and said that at last she was free.

Val had always been rather nervous of her, but the recent Mud-and-Bill-Bridge experience had left her feeling grown up and worldly wise. She thought it would be very nice to see how Theo was getting on, and to ask whether she needed any help with anything. After all, families were very important.

She found her sitting on the floor in a big bare room, eating a marmalade sandwich and listening to a record-player. The music was so loud that it seemed to jump off the walls.

'Hullo, Theo. How are you?' mouthed Val.

'Okay. You?' Theo mouthed back.

As she made no attempt to switch off the music they had to wait until the record ended. By this time Theo had finished her sandwich and Val had had time to contemplate her appearance, which was different from last time.

Then, Theo had had hardly any hair; the brown fuzz that had escaped the clippers had covered her scalp like moss on a gravestone, and she had had a small colourful bird tattooed on her forehead. But now her hair was Mohican and in black and pink stripes, and circles of matching pink had been painted on each cheekbone. She was wearing a magenta satin evening skirt, so old that it was practically fancy dress, and over the top of it a man's shirt with the collar and sleeves torn off. One bare arm was painted blue and the other lime green and

47

Val thought the result startling but undeniably beautiful.

In the silence left by the music Theo sat licking the butter off her fingers. 'Drink?'

'What sort?' Val asked cautiously.

'Tea. Got no milk.'

'No, thanks. I'm okay.'

'So what's up?'

'Oh, nothing's up. I just thought I'd call and see you, that's all.'

Without replying, Theo got up from the floor and went over to the Sainsbury's carrier bag lying in the empty hearth. From it she extracted a sliced loaf, a wodge of butter and a jar of marmalade and proceeded to make herself another sandwich.

'What happened to your bird?' Val asked.

'Bird?'

'Your tattoo.'

'Transfer,' Theo said, slapping two slices of bread together. 'Not tattoo.'

'Oh. Well, it was nice.'

Theo grunted, and came back with her sandwich. She sat down with her bare feet tucked under her skirt, then reached across to the record-player.

'Can't we talk?' Val shouted above the music.

'What about?'

That's a point, thought Val. What about? Is she as strictly non-chatty with everyone, or is it just me?

'I'm in the school swimming team —'

'Uh?'

'I said I'm . . . Oh, never mind.' Val leaned back against the wall feeling a bit fed up. The music

48

pounded on, and Theo's eyes took on a glazed look. She munched her sandwich as if she didn't realize she was doing so.

'Tell me what you've been up to, then.' Val shrieked a last attempt. 'How you've been getting on, and everything.'

But her voice was lost in the savage sound beating the air. It made the window rattle, and fine dust rose from the floor as if invisible people were dancing.

Now fed up beyond caring, Val prepared to depart, and just then the record ended. Theo looked like someone who had just returned from a long way off.

'I'm going now.'

'Uh-huh.' Then as if suddenly aware of her sister's presence, Theo added: 'What did you come for?'

'To see you, of course.'

'Did *they* send you?'

'Who – Mud and Father? Oh no, no, I just came because I wanted to.'

'Because, listen, I'm not into the family bit. I'm not into friendly chat and the cosy sister scene. It cramps me like I'm in some sort of prison cell and I want out.'

'Yes –'

'People are always trying to mess with your identity –' Theo had come to life now.

'I wasn't – honestly. I was just –'

'People have got to accept me on my terms and nobody else's. I'm *me*.'

'Yes, I know you are –'

'And I'm going to stay being *me*. Being *me*'s very important to me –'

'I suppose it is to everyone,' Val said from over by the door. 'Goodbye, Theo.'

Going downstairs she passed open doorways and caught glimpses of other strange and colourful people, and wondered if they were all equally determined not to have their identities messed with.

She began to walk home. It was a long way, but meandering along looking in shop windows and dreaming about things was very pleasant. She stopped thinking about Theo and began to dream about being school swimming champion, then saw a little pair of blue earrings in Woolworths, and as they only cost fifty pence she bought them for Mud. The sun was hot, and she sat on a bench outside a church admiring the earrings and dreaming some more about the swimming gala. Everyone would be watching. And everyone meant not only Alice and the other girls but, most important of all, the family.

And the thought of the family brought her back to reality. She hadn't told anyone she was going to see Theo – had forgotten even to mention that she was going out – and the clock on the church told her that she was already over an hour late for lunch.

Oh no, Mud would be furious. Hastily shoving the earrings back in her pocket, she set off for the nearest bus stop, then realized that she had only a couple of coppers left. She began to run, slowed to a jog, then, as the stitch in her side got worse, had to make do with walking.

It was half past two when she reached home. Putting on a last tired spurt she rushed into the kitchen and sank down on to a chair.

'I *am* sorry – didn't notice the time –'

The kitchen looked very clean and tidy. It was also unusually quiet. And the only person in it was Father, who was standing in the middle of it with his back to her. He turned round very slowly when he heard Val, and she couldn't get over how strange he looked. Pale and ill and sort of wrung out.

'Mud's run away,' he said.

# CHAPTER FOUR

Not just the kitchen but the whole house was silent, as if the spring had run down and there was no one to rewind it.

'She *can't* have!'

'Yes, she has. I've just said so.'

'Was it with —?' Val stopped, unable to say his name.

'With who?'

'I — oh, nothing . . .'

She couldn't say any more. All she could do was sit there, dry-mouthed and blank-eyed, and when Sheepshanks crept from under the table and put his cold damp nose in her hand, she shivered violently.

'What'll we do?'

'The best we can, I suppose.' Father came over and pulled another chair out from the table. He sat down heavily. 'I don't know what happened — well, that's just it, nothing happened so far as I'm concerned. I went down to the garage to buy a can of petrol for the mower, had a chat with someone I knew, and when I got back there was this note on the table.' He fumbled in his pocket.

'Shall I read it?' In a way, she didn't want to.

'You might as well. It concerns you as much as me.'

Reluctantly Val unfolded the piece of paper and smoothed it flat.

Lunch in oven. Clean shirts in airing cupboard. Milk bill paid. Don't try to find me because it won't work. I've made up my mind. Sheepshanks' worm pills in 2nd drawer from left in dresser. Due for one in 3 weeks.

'She seems to have thought of everything,' Val said lamely.

'But all such daft things!' Father cried, suddenly angry. 'As if worm pills and clean shirts matter a damn compared with her running away! I mean, what are we going to do? How are we supposed to survive? I'm at work, you're at school, the twins can't be left – who's going to see to everything?'

He pushed his chair back and began to tramp up and down the kitchen.

'Where are the twins now?'

'Search me.'

'Did they have any lunch?'

'Yes, they cleaned up the lot. I didn't feel hungry.'

'Have you told them about Mud?'

Father stopped tramping and came back to the table. 'No, not exactly. I just said she'd gone out for a while.'

'Perhaps that's all she has done,' Val said, trying to sound comforting. 'Perhaps she'll feel different after a couple of hours and come home again. I mean, when it gets to bedtime . . .'

And the thought of bedtime made her eyes fill with tears. Bending her head low she groped in her skirt pocket for a handkerchief, but of course she hadn't got one. She sniffed.

'Don't cry, Val.'

'But it'll be so lonely. So awful . . .'

'I know. But we're not the only ones it's happened to.'

'That doesn't make it any better . . .' Her tears increased as she remembered about Janice Brewer's mother running off with a man called Harry. She also remembered how smug Alice had been about self-centred parents and about the divorce rate being one in three.

'Here —' Father tore a square of paper towel from the roll and handed it to her, 'dry your eyes and cheer up. If you fall apart, I'll do the same.'

'Sorry.' She scrubbed her cheeks and then blew her nose. She managed a damp smile. 'So long as you don't run away, too.'

'I'm only running as far as the study,' he said, sighing. 'I've got a pile of essays to mark before Monday.'

Alone in the horribly quiet and tidy kitchen Val tried to get used to the idea of Mud not being there any more. Of her being with Bill Bridge instead of them. She pictured her ironing his shirts, making his meals, going to bed with him instead of Father, and she began to feel angrier than she had ever done in her life. What *right* had she? How dared she be so selfish and mean and rotten? . . . Pictures of Mud and Bill Bridge danced before her eyes and she felt the same kind of angry pain that had made Father tramp up and down the kitchen.

She began to do the same, and reaching the shelf where the glass jar of biscuits stood, realized that she had had no lunch. But she wasn't hungry. The shock of Mud's running away had killed her appetite just as effectively as it had killed Father's. Perhaps their appetites would never come back and they would die of *anorexia nervosa*, which was what a girl at school had.

She tried desperately hard to cheer up, and almost succeeded, but when she remembered Father's passionate cry: *'How are we supposed to survive?'* she started to cry all over again and this time she couldn't stop.

It was without exception the most awful day of her life.

'I'm seeing you into bed tonight because Mud's had to go away,' Val said later that day.

Pyjama'd and dressing-gowned, the twins hurtled upstairs from their supper and flung themselves in a fighting, giggling, tangling mass on their bedroom floor.

'Did you hear what I said?' Val followed them. 'Mud's had to go away.'

She had spent a lot of time pondering the best way of breaking the news to them, and had come to the conclusion that by bending the truth just a little she could make it sound far less upsetting. 'Mud has *had* to go away' suggested that she'd gone on an errand of mercy somewhere, and would soon be back. She had rehearsed saying it all through their bath and supper and was ready to cuddle them when they burst into tears, but she needn't have bothered.

'Ranko ranko gibbish!' shrieked Bertie, sitting astride Bardo's chest.

'Gibbish nonna ranko!' Bardo shrieked back, and wriggling from under his brother, seized his foot and bit it. They formed themselves into a fresh tangle of flailing limbs and breathless giggles, and Val set about folding up their jeans and tee-shirts in silence.

The twins had each other. They had their own games, their own language, their own world, and they didn't really need anyone else.

But after she'd hauled them apart, sent them to clean their teeth and then brushed their thickets of hair down flat, they lay in their side-by-side twin beds and stared at her attentively.

'Where's Mud?'

'I told you. She's had to go away for a little while.'

'Where?'

'To see a friend. Who's ill.'

'Is it nice, seeing people who are ill?'

'Not particularly. But it's nice *of* people to go and see them.'

'Why?'

'Well, because – they go to see if there's anything they can do to help.'

'Who is it who's ill?' Bardo asked.

'No one you know.'

'Will they die?'

'I don't know,' Val said. 'We'll have to wait and see.'

She kissed them goodnight, smoothed their covers, adjusted the window blind and went downstairs.

'Your mother and I were supposed to be going out to drinks this evening,' Father said. 'I suppose I'll have to ring them up and cancel it.'

'Can't you go on your own?'

'Well, I could, but they'll ask me where she is and I can't very well tell them she's run away.'

'Say she's got a cold, or something.'

Father grunted, and Val thought yes, I know. We can tell fibs for a while, but sooner or later everyone'll have to know.

'Tell them the truth then,' she suggested, 'and get it over with.'

He didn't answer, but a little while later she heard the *ting* of the telephone and then Father's voice saying: 'Awfully sorry, but . . .'

Which meant that he couldn't face them. A bit cowardly, Val thought, then changed her mind when she pictured how rotten it was going to be when she had to tell Alice and everybody.

So they spent the evening gloomily watching television, and just before she went up to bed Val said: 'I'll stay home from school on Monday to look after the boys. We'll be starting exams soon and there's lots of revision I can be doing.'

He gave her the sort of gentle smile he generally reserved for Mud, and just before she fell asleep Val got the feeling that somehow, some way, they would get through this awful time.

They got through Sunday fairly well. There were ready-cooked things in the freezer, the twins helped to make their own beds, and in the afternoon they all went up on the common with Sheepshanks, who craftily made friends with a tiny girl in a pushchair and then stole her woolly rabbit.

It took a long while to persuade him to give it up, and when Val finally returned it, the little girl's mother said: 'I don't fancy it now he's had it in his mouth, so he'd better keep it.' So Sheepshanks carried it all the way home and then carefully buried it in his basket among all the other treasures.

But Monday was different. With no one at home to back her up, Val found it difficult to restrain Bardo and Bertie from turning their bedroom into Houston Space Centre (with lift-off through the window), and from trying to make bricks from soil and water in the bathroom washbasin, and when she lost her temper and slapped them for lighting a fire in the garage they slapped her back and told her that she was a horrible old *thing* . . .

But apart from the twins it was so desperately boring, and the day seemed endless. She tried to do some revision but her mind kept sliding away, so she wandered round the house, upstairs, downstairs, and then out into the garden, where the sun was hot and the flowers were drooping because there was no Mud to water them.

The one thing she would have loved to do was to go swimming. Staring at a history textbook she imagined the cool dappled water lapping her shoulders, the stinging fountain of bubbles as she dived . . . but of course she couldn't leave the twins. She wondered if Rob Lacey would miss going swimming with her after school. Wondered whether he would miss her, full stop. Because she couldn't see how she would ever go back to school now that she had the twins to look after, plus Father and the house . . . The careless schoolgirl Val of last week already seemed centuries away.

Then Bertie fell down and cut his knee. It bled quite a lot, and when Val hurried him indoors and tried to bathe it, the disinfectant in the water made it hurt more than ever and his roars of pain changed to anguished sobs at the idea of anyone being so cruel and heartless.

'But I've got to clean the dirt out, Bertie, otherwise it'll go septic –'

'You're hurting it! – you're hurting it *worse*!'

'I know I am, but it's only for a *minute*!'

Then Bertie looked round the kitchen with streaming eyes and suddenly cried: 'Where's Mud? I want Mud! . . .' It was as if he had just noticed her absence.

'She's coming back – she won't be long. Look, hold your knee still . . .'

But it was no use. Like a poor little animal needing the warm comfort of its mother, Bertie cried helplessly, heartbrokenly, and, immediately infected by his sorrow, Bardo joined in. Their tears blended and ran together.

'Where's Mu-mu-mud? Why doesn't Mu-mud come? We don't want you, we want *her* . . .'

'She's coming back soon!' Val shouted above the noise, then the basin of water and disinfectant slipped from her lap and smashed on the floor.

And when she looked up, she saw a strange woman standing in the doorway.

'Oh dear,' the woman said. 'Can I help?'

For one dizzying second they all thought that perhaps it was Mud after all, but of course it wasn't. It was nothing like her. This woman had short grey hair (not red), and a big nose, and they had never seen her before in their lives. The twins stopped sobbing in mid-hiccup, and they all stared at her.

'The garden gate was on the latch,' the woman said. 'I knocked on the door but I don't think you heard.'

Then she came forward, and avoiding the puddle of water and the pieces of broken basin, swiftly examined Bertie's knee, exclaimed in admiration of his marvellous bravery, then dabbed it dry with a clean handkerchief and tied it round.

'There now,' she said. 'What a good thing I called to see if there was anything I could do.'

It was suddenly a huge relief to have a grown-up offering support, but for some reason she couldn't explain, Val found herself refusing it.

'There isn't anything that needs doing,' she said. Then added: 'Thank you, all the same.'

'Wouldn't you like me to look after the boys?'

'No, it's all right, thanks.'

'But what about you going to school?' The woman stooped to pick up the fragments of basin. 'And what about swimming?'

60

Val didn't know what to say. Worried and confused, she took the bits of broken basin from her and dropped them in the pedal bin.

It was Bardo who finally put into words the questions that were worrying his sister; looking up at the woman with wide unblinking eyes, he came straight to the point: 'Who are you? Where have you come from, and what do you want?'

'My name is Mrs Forrest,' the woman said, smiling down at him. 'I've come in my little car and I want to help to look after you, if your sister agrees.'

'How d'you know we want help?' Val asked. 'Who told you?'

'Let's just say I heard a rumour. Now, where's the floorcloth and I'll wipe up this puddle of water.'

Val fetched it from the cupboard under the sink. 'Are you from the Council, or something?'

The woman called Mrs Forrest laughed, and it was quite a jolly sound. 'Goodness me, no! I'm just a friend.'

'But we've never met you before.' Declining Mrs Forrest's help, Val mopped the puddle herself.

'I'm an old friend of your parents, and I haven't seen them for a long time. I haven't seen you since you were quite a baby, so of course I haven't seen the boys at all. Do you mind telling me which is which?'

'I'm Bertram,' said Bertie, 'and he's Bardolph.' Although their tears had dried, they still had a sort of lost orphan look.

'It must be very difficult for people to tell you

61

apart,' Mrs Forrest said. 'Perhaps you should always wear a bandage round your knee, Bertie!'

'It's really best if you treat them as one single person,' Val explained. 'That's what suits them best of all.'

The woman called Mrs Forrest seemed interested, and was nice, and when she smiled her nose didn't look so big. She suggested that it might be a good idea to have a cup of tea, so Val made one, and they took it out in the garden on a tray, with orange juice for the twins, and sat under the apple tree. And although Bardo had no bandage round his knee, he walked with the same stiff-legged gait as his brother.

'I see what you mean about them being like one person,' Mrs Forrest said. Then turned her attention to Val. 'I hear you're a very good swimmer.'

'I'm in the school team and the gala's in two weeks' time,' Val said. Then added: 'How did you know I like swimming?'

'Oh, I must have heard it somewhere,' Mrs Forrest said vaguely, then changed the subject. 'My goodness, those poor petunias want watering, don't they?'

'Yes. My mother generally does it, but –' Val bit her tongue, unwilling to talk about private family affairs.

But it seemed as if Mrs Forrest hadn't heard, because all she said was: 'Tell me where the watering can is and I'll do them.'

'Actually, we have a hose,' Bardo said.

'All the better. Come on, show me where it is.'

They went with her to the garden shed and Val

stayed under the apple tree thinking that Mrs Forrest had got a bit of a cheek, making herself at home like that.

But it had to be admitted that she knew how to keep the twins happy. She had exactly the right sort of knack. Although playing with the hose was normally forbidden, she allowed them to spray the flowers and then the lettuces and tomato plants, and when Bertie accidentally sprayed her as well, she didn't seem to mind.

'Would you like to come and spend the day with me tomorrow?' she asked them, when they came back to where Val was sitting.

They said that they would, and she said that she had a big telescope that had once belonged to her husband.

'Why doesn't it belong to him now?'

'Because he's dead.'

'Oh,' said Bertie. 'Are you going to get another one?'

'What – husband?' Mrs Forrest began to laugh. 'I don't know, I might do.'

'Otherwise it's a waste of a telescope,' Bardo said.

They stayed there chatting easily and happily in the sweet smell of wet earth and grateful plants, and Val very, very nearly liked Mrs Forrest but not quite. There was something mysterious about the way she had suddenly arrived – like the fairy godmother in a pantomime – and Val had a feeling that she might turn out to be bossy.

Sure enough, she asked Val what she was planning to cook for supper.

'Toad-in-the-hole,' said Val, who in fact hadn't planned anything at all.

'Oh dear, won't that be rather heavy for a warm summer evening?'

'This is a special light recipe. It came from my grandmother.'

'It sounds as if you're a good little cook.'

'It's one of my best subjects,' Val said, resenting the word *little*.

Then Father appeared, loosening his tie and saying how hot it had been in town. He paused, and looked puzzled when he saw Mrs Forrest.

'Hello, Paul,' she said, and shook his hand. 'You don't remember me, do you?'

'I'm afraid I . . .' Father looked gently vague.

'We met many years ago . . . I have a sister called Lilian who writes poetry . . .'

'Yes, of course!' Father said with a heartiness that didn't sound altogether genuine. 'I remember her very well. *And* you . . . Is there any tea left, Val?'

Val went to fetch another cup and saucer, and returned in time to hear Mrs Forrest saying: 'Oh no, I don't write poetry – I'm not nearly clever enough. After my husband died I had to earn a little money, and so I became a home knitter.'

A home knitter, thought Val, pouring out the tea, which was almost cold. What sort of person would live in a knitted home? Knitted walls, knitted ceilings . . . she can't mean it . . .

'I knit at home,' Mrs Forrest was saying to Father. 'Jumpers and cardigans and shawls for babies. It's very convenient, but I do get a bit lonely sometimes.'

'Then you must come and see us more often,' Father said, and Val could tell that he still had no idea who Mrs Forrest was. 'My wife and I would be delighted to –'

He stopped suddenly, and there was an awkward silence. Not only had he forgotten Mrs Forrest, he had even forgotten, temporarily, that Mud had run away.

'My wife is on holiday at the moment,' he said, 'but as soon as she returns we will be delighted to –'

'Have you for supper,' put in Bertie.

'*To* supper,' Father corrected automatically.

'I would really look forward to that, Paul,' Mrs Forrest said. And the slow, strange smile she gave Father seemed to go on and on, like a rich sunset.

'Listen, you remember about Janice Brewer's mother running away with another man,' Val said to Alice next day.

'Yes. His name was Harry.'

'Well, how's her father getting on? I mean, is he lonely and fed up all on his own?'

'I haven't heard anything definite,' Alice said, 'but it strikes me he must be. Although he's still got Janice, of course.'

'But Janice isn't the same as a grown-up woman, is she?'

'No. Not yet.' Then Alice dropped her prim look and turned to stare hard at Val. 'Anyway, what's made you so interested in Janice's father?'

'Nothing,' said Val, going pink. 'I just wondered, that's all.'

65

Thanks to Mrs Forrest's offer to take the twins, Val had gone back to school (bearing a note from Father to say that on the previous day she had suffered from toothache, which was now better), and although she wasn't looking forward to the exams, it was nice to be back. It was also nice to know that Alice was Speaking, but all the same she had no intention of telling her about Mud. Or about Mrs Forrest, although there wasn't very much to tell about her; at least, not so far.

As Mrs Forrest had promised to bring the twins home at five o'clock there was no time to go swimming in the lake at Beauchamp Park, but she met Rob on the way to the pool attached to the sports centre.

'Not long before the gala,' he said, falling into step beside her.

'Think our school'll win?'

'I think we'll do well in the relay, at least.'

'I'm getting more jittery about the swimming than I am about the exams, and that's saying something.'

'You've no need to be,' Rob said. 'You're one of our brightest hopes.'

'That makes me jitter worse than ever,' Val told him. But she was very pleased, all the same. The dream of being school champion came back, stronger than ever, and it helped to blot out the misery about Mud and the worry about the future.

Nearly all the school team was at the pool, and under the eye of Mr Cook, the swimming coach, Val practised back crawl and the five basic springboard dives. Although he didn't say much she could tell that he was pleased with her, and the thought made her glow with happiness all the way home.

But the glow stopped when she went into the kitchen and found Father and Mrs Forrest drinking tea and eating ginger cake and chatting as if they were really close friends.

Both twins were sitting at the table with them, busily colouring the pictures in bright new colouring books. Bardo looked up at her for a moment.

'This woman's really nice,' he said. 'She let us look through her telescope and she bought us these books. *And* these crayons.'

'This woman has a name,' Father said. 'It's Mrs Forrest.'

'Hello, Val,' Mrs Forrest said, smiling. 'Had a good day at school?'

'Yes, thank you.'

But Mrs Forrest went on looking at her, and gradually her smile faded to an expression of concern. 'Val – is there something wrong?'

'Yes,' Val said in a stiff, prim little voice like Alice's. 'You're sitting in my mother's chair.'

# CHAPTER FIVE

But whether she liked it or not, that was the new régime.

From Monday to Friday Mrs Forrest looked after the twins so that Val could go to school. Mostly she collected them and took them to her own home, but sometimes she stayed on with them at the Hopes' house, and those were the times that Val resented most of all.

'There's no need for you to do our ironing,' she said. 'I can do it myself.'

'But I've nothing better to do,' Mrs Forrest would smile. 'I get tired of knitting, and it seems silly just to sit here and do nothing.'

As well as the ironing, she also mended things; sewed buttons on, patched and darned holes, and even retacked the lining of the sitting-room curtains, which had been hanging down ever since Val could remember.

It looked much better tacked up, but they were Mud's curtains, not hers, and she had no right to interfere.

Sometimes in the evenings Val tried to talk to Father about Mud, but he always seemed curiously unwilling.

'Why doesn't she even write to us? Or has she? — and you've not told me?'

'No,' he said. 'She hasn't written.'

Silence for ten minutes, while Val fiddled with a bit of French translation that wouldn't come right.

'Couldn't we get the police to look for her?'

'No, Val.'

'But why not?'

'Because you can't treat a grown-up woman like an inanimate object, as if she were a lost umbrella, or even Sheepshanks.'

'Sheepshanks isn't an inanimate object!'

'He might just as well be, so far as lack of brain goes.'

'That's my trouble,' Val said mournfully. 'I haven't got much brain either.'

'There's nothing wrong with your brain,' Father replied. 'Your trouble is that you don't always know how to use it.'

Val remained silent for a while, then said: 'But surely the law or something could make Mud come home? I mean, what about marriage vows, and all that?'

'Marriage vows are morally but not legally binding,' Father said, 'and there's a word for forcing people to live where they don't want to; it's *imprisonment*.'

'Well, then, can't we *persuade* her?'

'Not without knowing where she is.'

More silence. The new, deeply fed-up sort of silence that had crept all round the house now that Mud had gone. Val went back to her translation but

69

the sentence still wouldn't make sense. So she laid down her pen and said: 'I don't like Mrs Forrest very much.'

'Mrs Forrest is being very kind.' Father concealed himself behind the evening paper. 'The twins like her very much.'

'Yes, I know they do. But they're only little, and they don't notice other people like –'

'Like you do?'

Val didn't say anything. But she wished she could talk to him about noticing people so much more these days; *noticing* perhaps wasn't the right word – it was more like colliding with them. Once upon a time adults had been no more than a vague and pleasant blur, but now they seemed to be coming so much closer, getting so much more real, like pictures coming into focus.

'You're growing up, Val, that's the trouble,' Father said, as if he understood without her saying anything. He came out from behind the paper and smiled at her and it was like a gentle gleam of light on a cold dark day.

It made her want to say something comforting and loving to him in return, but once again the words wouldn't come. So she bent her head over her homework and clenched her hands tightly in her lap as if sheer physical effort would make the translation come out right. *There's nothing wrong with your brain*, he had said, which was at least encouraging.

She was on her way to bed when he followed her out into the hall. 'Oh, Val, I almost forgot. Your mother and I had invited some people round to

70

supper this Saturday – only four of them – d'you think you could cope?'

'You mean – cook it?' Her eyes opened wide with alarm.

'You wouldn't have to fuss – something quite plain and simple is all we need.'

'Well, I'll try.' She stood looking at him from the foot of the stairs. 'Do they know about Mud?'

'Not the details. I've just said she's away for a time.'

'I see.'

'Which is a bit feeble of me, I suppose.'

'I haven't told my friends either,' Val said. 'Not yet.'

'Which makes us a couple of old feeblies together, doesn't it?'

They said goodnight, then before going back into the sitting room he called up to her: 'They're very nice people who are coming. Colleagues from work – incidentally, one of them's married to someone from your school . . .'

'Don't worry,' she said. 'We'll manage okay.' It was nice to be able to say something comforting and loving after all.

'How's your mother's sculpture?' Alice asked, on the way to the bus stop.

'It's fine.'

'What's she making?'

'She's making –' Val drew a deep breath, 'a statue of my father.'

'What – lifesize?'

71

'Oh yes, naturally. When my mother starts something she does it properly.'

'Hmm,' said Alice.

The bus had arrived and they were sitting in it side by side when Val looked out of the window and suddenly saw Bill Bridge walking along the pavement. He was walking briskly, threading his way through the afternoon shoppers, and the sight of him made her heart begin to thump violently.

Without bothering to think, she shoved past Alice and jumped off the bus when it paused at the traffic lights. Several drivers hooted at her as she dashed towards the kerb, yet by the time she reached it Bill Bridge was a long way in front of her. She could just see his wavy fair hair above the heads of the crowd.

She hurried on, dodging from side to side and occasionally banging into people, then he turned into a side road and when she reached it she just had time to see him slam the door of a red Fiesta before driving away.

She stood there, panting and watching the brake lights flick on at the far end of the street, and she realized then that she had no idea what she had intended to do, supposing she had caught up with him. Demand the return of Mud forthwith? Even hit him, maybe?

She walked the rest of the way home deep in thought. Supposing she called at the place where he taught, asked to see him in private and then pleaded with him to give Mud back to the family? It seemed like a good idea, but there were difficulties; calling there during daytime classes would mean skipping school and the exams were about to start, and in the evening she might run the risk of seeing him there with Mud herself. Visions of Bill Bridge teaching Mud the art of sculpture with one arm round her waist filled Val with a kind of squeamish horror. She came to the conclusion that she didn't want to see Mud at all, unless it was back home where she belonged.

She decided to ring Bill Bridge up, and spent a tormented half hour plucking up courage to dial the number she found listed in the book while Father was in the study. But the B. Bridge turned out to be a lady called Beatrice, and by the time that Val had worked out that Bill would be under W for William — the last of her courage had seeped away. Then it occurred to her that Mud herself might well have answered the phone supposing she had dialled the right number, and that she would probably have made a worse mess of talking to her than to Bill Bridge.

She didn't know what to do for the best, so, like Father, she did nothing. And in the meanwhile they had the first of the exams, which was algebra, and afterwards, when she compared the answers with Alice, Val discovered that most of hers were wrong. (At any rate, they were different.)

'Still, we can't all be good at everything, can we?' said Mrs Forrest soothingly when Val, longing for a bit of sympathy, confided the dismal facts over a cup of tea.

'But everyone's bright in our family but me.'

'I think you're very bright,' Mrs Forrest said. 'But even more important, I think you're very nice.'

'Do you honestly?' Val was taken aback. Her cheeks flared deep pink.

'Yes. I think you're very kind and loyal and thoughtful and loving. As a matter of fact,' Mrs Forrest said with her face turned away, 'I always wanted to have a daughter like you.'

'Like me? Honestly?' Val's pink deepened to a grand beetroot red. 'But I'm so ordinary . . .'

'And one of the good qualities I forgot to mention,' Mrs Forrest said, 'is that you're such a modest, self-effacing girl.'

Perhaps it was just as well that the twins came in then. They came up to Val in one of their rare moods of affection, and rubbed themselves against her like two charming tee-shirted kittens.

'If you like,' they said to her, 'you can be the king of Them. But we won't shoot you because you're really quite a nice sort of king.'

'As Val is your sister, shouldn't you make her queen?' Mrs Forrest suggested, and for the first time since her arrival the twins treated her to their special brand of disdainful pity.

'Queens,' Bardo said, 'don't generally *do* much.'

'The thing is,' Val felt bound to explain when they were out of earshot, 'they're really too young to know the difference between male and female.'

'If only we could all be like that,' Mrs Forrest sighed. 'What a happy place the world would be.'

Her words brought back the shadow of Mud and Bill Bridge; of Janice Brewer's mother and the haulage contractor called Harry. And in a way it was just as well, because Val discovered that she was in danger of getting to like Mrs Forrest.

All the same, it was a bad moment when Father broke the news that the colleague who was married to someone from Val's school was a chap called Farthing.

'Oh no – not *Farthing*!'

'Yes. Why, what's the matter?'

With sleeves rolled up, hair flopping in her eyes, fingers slippery with butter, sticky with pastry, dusty with flour, and with the rest of her smelling of raw onions, Val said: 'Mrs Farthing's our cookery teacher.'

'What a super coincidence,' Father said encouragingly. 'She'll be able to give you a hand if you get in a muddle.'

Val said nothing, but went on trying to mould the pastry into a lump that could be rolled out. It seemed to prefer collapsing in a heap of crumbs.

'What are you making us?' Father peered at it.

'Shepherd's pie and lemon meringue,' Val said defensively. 'You said to make it simple.'

'Sounds jolly good. What to start with?'

'Well,' his daughter raised harassed eyes. 'I suppose we could have grapefruit.'

'Better and better!' Father rubbed his hands. 'Let me know if there's anything I can do to help.'

'There is something,' Val said. 'You could take the boys out for a walk, because they keep wanting to come in and give me advice.'

He did so, but being left alone with the cooking didn't seem to make it any easier, for there had been a certain amount of exaggeration on Val's part when she told Mrs Forrest that cookery was one of her best subjects. It was, in fact, one of her worst. Worse than French, worse than maths, and even worse than English. As for her relationship with Mrs Farthing, it had slumped to an all-time low after a long summer term of particularly awful culinary disasters ('But how did a drawing pin come to *be* in your Victoria sandwich, Valeria? . . .'). To Val, the thought of her coming to supper was as terrible as the time they told her she needed to have her tonsils out.

But she plodded on, and after several attempts to roll the pastry into a manageable slab, lost her temper with it and poured the crumbs into the dish and then hammered them down flat with her fist.

Returning from their walk the twins were annoyed to discover that their presence would not be required that evening, but agreed to settle for watching *Drums of Wrath* on the portable TV when they were in bed.

'Is Mud coming to supper, too?'

'No, I don't think so.'

'Why? Doesn't she like the other people who are coming?'

'I don't know. I expect she does.'

'Then *why* isn't she coming?'

'Because –' the hiss of a boiling saucepan sent Val leaping for the stove. 'Oh . . . because she's having supper with King Hussein –'

'Who's King –?'

'Look, for heaven's sake get *lost*, can't you!'

76

'Very well, if that's how you feel,' Bertie said. 'But it may interest you to know that Sheepshanks has been sniffing your shepherd's pie.'

By seven-thirty the dining table had been laid, the sitting room tidied, and Val had changed out of her jeans into a yellow striped dress that she didn't particularly like, but which felt suitable. She was brushing her hair when her gaze fell upon a small paper bag tucked in the corner of her open dressing-table drawer. She took it out, shook it, and the pair of blue earrings she had bought for Mud tumbled into her lap.

She sat looking at them and thinking that they would have suited Mud like anything. Brushing her hair back she held them against her ears, then on impulse clipped them on. They made her feel adult, and pleasingly poised.

Downstairs in the sitting room Father was humming a tune and polishing the sherry glasses.

'Everything under control, Val?'

'It was, the last time I looked. Trouble with cooking is that it keeps on changing all the time.'

She wondered whether he would notice the earrings, or comment about the extra pains she had taken with her appearance. But he didn't. He just went on humming and looking happy, and Val supposed that it was a good thing he had cheered up about Mud and everything.

When the doorbell rang he went to answer it, and Val suffered a sudden attack of mortal terror when she heard Mrs Farthing's voice in the hall. Stifling a mad desire to bury her head in a cushion, she squared her shoulders and did her best to prepare a smooth, calm smile of welcome.

'Hello, Valeria,' Mrs Farthing said, wearing an even smoother, calmer smile. She was also wearing a sleeveless dress with a low neckline and her hair tizzled up in little curls which made her look quite a bit younger and prettier. But she was still Mrs Farthing, Cookery Teacher and Head of Dom. Science.

'Hello, Mrs Farthing,' Val said, then found her hand being shaken with great heartiness by Mrs Farthing's husband, a large bald man in horn-rims.

The other couple arrived, whose name was Briggs, and it was a relief that they all knew each other and didn't just stand there staring at Val's (Mud's) earrings and not saying anything. Father dispensed glasses of sherry while Val handed round the salted peanuts and Mr Briggs started to talk about his tomato plants, which had got brown root rot.

'Are you going to try a spot of sherry, Val?'

'I don't think so –'

'Go on, do you good.' Father was smiling his dear old loving smile, so she took a glass from him and ventured a small sip. It tasted like trifle without the sponge-cake.

They were all very nice to her, and included her in the conversation as if she were an adult. No one mentioned Mud, but Mrs Briggs chatted to her about playing in a tennis club tournament and seemed very interested when Val told her about the swimming gala.

'Not long now before the end of exams and the

end of term, eh, Valeria?' smiled Mrs Farthing, and smiling back at her Val wondered whether she already knew the results of the cookery exam. (She was bound to come bottom as usual, for Bakewell tart is rarely improved by being dropped on the floor and hastily shovelled back into its container, although Alice said she didn't think Mrs Farthing had noticed.)

'Yes . . .' Val said to Mrs Farthing, and because she couldn't think of anything else, raised her glass and said: 'Cheers!'

'Cheers!' responded Mrs Farthing, and Val began to relax until it slowly dawned on her that she was responsible for announcing when supper was ready.

She had seen Mud do it so many times; laughing, careless, graceful, and telling everyone where to sit and making jokes while Father poured the wine. She had always made everything look so easy. And such fun.

Val went out to the kitchen. The shepherd's pie was keeping warm in the oven, so she put the frozen peas on to cook. The lemon meringue looked quite nice although it was a little different from the usual recipe. Everything was ready except the peas, and the idea was that they should cook for the few minutes it would take them all to eat their grapefruit.

So she ought to go and call them. Now. *Supper's ready*! — nothing to it, but paralysed with nerves she hid her face in the roller towel and thought with agony of all the ghastly muck-ups she'd made during the course of her life. Tonight's supper, she was convinced, was going to be the most spectacular one of all.

But somehow she pulled herself together, and drawing a deep breath marched resolutely back to the sitting room and called: 'Supper's ready!' in a pretty fair imitation of Mud.

Only trouble was, they were now all chatting so hard that no one heard her.

Funnily enough, the worst part was the grapefruit, because she hadn't cut through the segments properly. Looking round the table she saw them all discreetly trying to hack through the membrane with their teaspoons, except for Father, who gave up and cheerfully crammed the whole stringy bunch of it into his mouth in one go. The juice ran down his chin and he beamed across at Val and said: '*Super* flavour! . . .'

Which helped her considerably. She removed the dishes and brought in the shepherd's pie, which, seen out of the oven, appeared more yellow than brown, but the pattern she had made in the potato with a fork still looked very nice. The peas had boiled a bit hard and jumped out of their jackets, but no one seemed to notice. They passed round the plates, and they smiled and they chatted and they ate, and then Mr Farthing raised his wine glass to Val and called out: 'Here's to Cookie!'

He asked Mrs Farthing whether Val was one of her pupils, and Mrs Farthing said yes, she was indeed.

'I bet she's streets ahead of all the others!' Mr Farthing said.

'She's certainly a very . . . challenging pupil,' his wife replied, and, crimson-cheeked, Val prayed that she would not encounter another drawing pin.

Although the potato had gone rather hard on top they ate all the shepherd's pie and finished the peas, and they were busily discussing the new Government White Paper on Education when Val brought in the lemon meringue.

Pausing in the act of opening another bottle of wine, Father asked why it had got cream on top instead of meringue, and they were all so nice to her that it was quite easy to take them into her confidence. Even Mrs Farthing.

'Well, you see,' she said, 'the egg whites wouldn't get stiff no matter how hard I beat them, so I threw them away and tried some more. They wouldn't get stiff either, although I went on and on and *on*, so in the end I thought oh, blow this, and threw them away too, and then I put cream on the top instead – which *did* beat up all right, so it must have been the eggs, not me. And as I didn't want to waste the four egg yolks from the second lot of eggs I beat them up and added them to the potato on top of the shepherd's pie. They've made it go a bit stiff and yellow-looking, but egg yolks –' and she gazed defiantly at Mrs Farthing – 'are, as we all know, a valuable source of vitamin B and should not, on that account alone, be wasted.'

'I must say your pastry's very short, Valeria,' Mrs

Farthing murmured, delicately pressing some on to the back of her fork.

'I once nearly married a woman whose pastry was incredibly *long*,' Father said, beaming happily. 'She had only to make sufficient pastry for an apple pie for two, and it would have stretched all the way from here to the Town Hall.'

'How very economical,' said Mr Briggs. 'What became of her?'

'Her name was Fanny,' Father said, pouring more wine, 'and she came to an unfortunate end, poor creature. Mistaking a bottle of lighter fuel for a bottle of Château Lafite she drank the lot and died of spontaneous combustion.'

They all laughed, and someone said thank goodness he'd married the right woman in the end.

'My wife is a paragon among women!' cried Father, draining his glass. 'She is a pearl beyond price, a treasure of inestimable value . . .' His gaiety increased. 'She is the salt of the earth, the pick of the bunch, a winner, a knockout, the greatest marvel since the invention of rubber gloves . . .'

Everyone was laughing, except Val. She wanted to, but couldn't. And it was because of a fumbling suspicion that Father was being funny at Mud's expense. Yes, okay, he knew a lot of words and could fire them off in brilliant showers like fireworks, but underneath all that she couldn't help feeling that he was really giving out the message that he didn't give two hoots for Mud any more than she gave two hoots for him, and that love and family ties and children and Sheepshanks and everything didn't matter any more than a dewdrop in a desert.

She sat looking down into her lap, conscious that Mud's earrings were pinching the lobes of her ears. And then suddenly remembered that it was time to bring in the biscuits and cheese.

'The origin of the word wedlock has nothing to do with locks and keys,' Father was saying when she returned. 'It derives from Old English, and the second syllable is taken from the word *lac*, meaning a promise . . .'

'Nothing to do with temporarily lacking a wife?' Mr Briggs inquired jokily.

'Have some cheese,' Val said.

But no one seemed to want any. They just sat there listening to Father being knowledgeable and funny about marriage ('And you know what Groucho Marx said about it – "Marriage is an institution, and who wants to live in an institution?" '). So Val just went on sitting there too, admiring him and feeling proud without understanding much because the words seemed to get longer and longer and the laughter louder and louder.

But very gradually the suspicion that he was being funny at Mud's expense became a certainty. He was betraying her, and no matter what Mud had done, it was wrong and cruel and rotten.

'Excuse me,' she said finally, in an Alice sort of voice. 'I'd better go and see if the twins are all right.'

She left the room without being noticed and went upstairs. The TV was still flickering to itself and the room was full of moonlight. She bent over each of the beds in turn, staring into the calm sleeping faces and thinking that's how I used to be; when I was their age I didn't notice grown-ups except as big forever-and-ever things in the background . . .

The earrings were pinching so hard now that they made her eyes water, so she took them off and put them in her pocket. She wondered whether anyone would miss her if she went to bed without saying goodnight, then remembered that as hostess she still had to supply the guests with coffee. So she went downstairs again, and through the open kitchen door heard Father leading them from the dining room to the sitting room.

She made the coffee and carried it in on a tray, and they were all having such a good time – Mrs Farthing with her shoes discreetly slipped off, Mr Briggs with cigar ash in his lap – that they didn't notice her at all. She might have been one of those machines you put money in, press a knob and the coffee pours itself out.

So she murmured goodnight and slipped quietly away, and even up in her bedroom she could hear the boom of Father's voice as he unleashed still more torrents of funny conversation. In the past it had been Mud who made all the noise and caused all the merriment, with Father no more than a courteous accompaniment, but now it was different. This was the new-type Father, sparkling with delight and whooping with laughter because his wife had left him. And because he was in love with Mrs Forrest.

She drifted off to sleep, then woke again. The

house was quiet now, and the moonlight had gone. She turned on her side, punching the pillow into a more comfortable position beneath her head, but sleep wouldn't return. The more she tried to persuade it, the more wide awake she became. Perhaps a drink of water would help.

She got out of bed and padded downstairs, and was surprised to see a shaft of light shining through the half-open study door. Her heart began to pound in case it was burglars. But it wasn't. It was Father, sitting with his back to her and his shoulders bowed, and he was weeping as if there was no earthly cure for the pain of his grief.

She stood in the doorway, deeply shocked because she had never seen a man cry before, and filled with despair because she didn't know the right words of comfort.

'Can I do anything to help? . . .' she whispered finally.

'No. Go to bed, Val,' he said in a harsh, ugly voice that she had never heard before. He remained with his back to her.

Helpless and miserable, she crept back to bed, and the only comfort she could find was to tell herself over and over again that grown-ups were really no more than big children.

# CHAPTER SIX

The exams were over, most of the results were out and most of them were bad except for dom. science (*Valeria is now showing signs of practical ability*, Mrs Farthing wrote, which was really big of her, considering) – and everyone was talking about where they were going for the holidays. No one seemed to be spending them at home except Val, and Alice was now beginning to show a marked curiosity about the affairs of the Hope family.

'Aren't you going away at *all*?'

'No. I've just told you.'

'We're going to Austria.'

'I know. You said.'

'How are your parents?'

'Fine. Why?'

'Oh – I just wondered. Janice says her father's fallen in love with someone else as well, now.'

'What's that got to do with me?'

'Nothing. Except that you were asking about him not long ago, so I thought you'd be interested.'

'Well, I'm not – see?'

'There's no need to snap. As a matter of fact Mummy wondered if you'd like to come home to supper tomorrow night.'

'No, thanks, I can't.'

'You haven't been for ages.'

'I know. I'm just a bit busy.'

'Doing what?'

'Oh – mind your own business!'

And Val slouched off scowling while Alice's little wise eyes watched and noted behind their spectacles.

Yet there were times when Val was strongly tempted to confide in her. To walk home with her through the quiet back streets and tell about Mud going off with Bill Bridge; and tell about the sudden and mysterious appearance of Mrs Forrest – *I think my father's been having an affair with her for a long while, and that before long she's going to move in and live with us . . .*

But the reason why she didn't say anything was now less to do with loyalty than with this new numb sort of feeling that grown-ups were stupid and boring and not worth getting upset about. She began to understand how Theo felt. I'm not into the family bit, Theo had said. I'm me. And Theo had got it right; probably she'd also been worried and hurt and embarrassed by Mud and Father at some stage in the past.

It wasn't the children's fault when parents behaved stupidly, and if they made themselves miserable in the process, well, it served them right; but it wasn't fair to make their children miserable as well. As for Father actually sitting there and crying – Val's pity was now hardening into a squeamish contempt, and there were times when she felt sure that he must read it in her eyes.

In the meanwhile she was polite to Mrs Forrest, adequate in her dealings with the twins and Sheep-shanks, and made a point of avoiding Father as much as she could. She became steadily more efficient at cooking meals and seeing to things in general, but if anyone said thank you to her for anything, she responded with no more than a brief and tight-lipped little smile. It was nothing like her old smile.

The moment I'm sixteen I'm leaving school, this new smile said. I'm clearing out, leaving home. I'm going to live like Theo does, because Theo's got it all worked out.

In the meantime summer term ended on Friday, and on the following day there was the swimming gala. She had done very little practice lately, and at one moment had even considered withdrawing from the team. But she had left it too late, and the only girl who could have replaced her had already gone off on holiday. So she turned up, and there was a funny sort of satisfaction in knowing that neither Father nor the twins would be there, because she hadn't invited them.

'I've got to go out on Saturday afternoon,' she had said. 'Can you look after the boys?'

'Yes, of course. Going anywhere nice?'

If he had been a more caring type of father he would have wanted to know all the details; would have insisted on the where and the why, and in the end she would have told him. And he would have insisted on coming to watch, and to cheer her on and be proud of her. But then, if he'd been a caring sort of father he would have remembered that it was the day of the swimming gala, anyway.

'No, not very nice,' she said. 'Just a boring old school thing.'

Even then, he didn't remember. At that moment she felt she hated him.

But as soon as she came barefoot out of the changing cubicle and smelt the sharp chlorine smell of the water, all thoughts of home and family disappeared. The old happy tingle of anticipation, mixed now with the excitement of competing in the team, made her jig up and down, and not once did she bother to glance up at the rows of spectators waiting for the opening event.

Rob was among the crowd of competitors clustering round the school swimming coach. He smiled and waved when he saw Val.

'Where've you been all this time?'

'Busy,' Val said, but this time with a grin.

'Hope you're feeling up to scratch –'

'Can't wait to get started!'

And from the fierce restless energy that filled her she knew that she was going to swim and dive better than she had ever done before. And she wouldn't be doing it for the family – she would be doing it for herself and for the school.

They began with the junior heats, and although she still wasn't looking up at it Val was aware of the parental cries of encouragement floating down from the spectators' gallery.

The team they were competing against was from

a neighbouring comprehensive, and it soon became clear that they were fairly evenly matched. The away school seemed strong on both breast and butterfly stroke, and the shouts and cries of encouragement coming from their supporters soared towards the glass dome of the roof. The supporters of Val's school became equally noisy, and towards the end of the 100 metres front crawl a deep fatherly voice roared out: *'Come on, Robbie boy!'* as Rob pounded along into second place.

Heats and finals followed each other in rapid and well-organized succession. The order to 'Take your marks' gave way to a few seconds of tense silence and then the crack of the starting pistol and the crash of water as the competitors sprang into action. Val's school was doing well, and just before she took her place for the finals of the back crawl race Rob touched her shoulder and said: 'You're going to win – easily.'

She jumped in, swam a few preparatory strokes then took her place by the bar, her feet braced against the tiles. The competitor in the next lane was a girl with cropped hair and powerful shoulders; they smiled at one another briefly, nervously, then they were on their marks – poised and motionless.

As the sound of the pistol hit the glass roof, Val threw her arms back and launched into the preliminary glide. The water closed over her head, plunging her into silence, then she broke surface and began swimming. It took her the first quarter-length to settle down from a furious explosion of energy to a steady rhythmical co-ordination of limbs. Each strong arm-pull was balanced by the downward kick of the opposite leg, and she remembered about swimming in a straight line by keeping a check on the glass roof sections above her head. As her ears lapped the water she heard snatches of cheers and exhortations coming from the spectators, and the thrashing of water from the competitors on both sides of her. Her breathing was good too – one breath with each arm movement – and she began to brace herself for the turn at the end of the pool.

Putting on speed she touched the wall, and then pulled her knees up and launched herself into the spin they had practised with Mr Cook.

Taking a quick gulp of air she dropped below the surface, felt the tiles against her feet, and shoved for all she was worth. She broke surface again and was away on the second half – back in the effort of lift-pull-kick-breathe – and when she suddenly became aware that there was no one swimming abreast of her in either lane, made a conscious effort to suppress elation by glancing up at the roof sections to check the straightness of her course.

And then she heard them cheering. Screaming, was more the word.

'Come on, Val! – Val – Val – come on!...' The voices broke against her eardrums every time her head lifted a fraction higher, then the water would blot them out again. But it was her name all right. *Val – Val – come on, Val!*

And she was swimming faster and better than she had ever done before. Almost as if she was in someone else's body. And her mind was so cool, too; it checked the point in the roof sections that told her she had four more arm movements to go before the end, and the voices rose in a great crescendo as she tore through the water and the fingers of her left hand touched the wall and she was home.

They cheered and clapped and roared, and she huddled down close to the rail, shaking her head and blinking as the other competitors came pounding in after her. They were announcing her name as she climbed out of the water and Mr Cook went over to her and congratulated her. She didn't think she had ever seen him look so pleased before.

'You really made your mind up to win, didn't you?' he said, heaping the big towel round her shoulders.

'Yes,' Val said. 'I did it for our school.'

When the races were finished they went on to the diving. The dives were mostly from the springboard and were, generally speaking, competent but unexciting. Only one boy from the other school attempted a somersault from the high board, and when Val's turn came she executed a couple of neat headers which drew more applause than they really deserved. It seemed as if everyone was still very pleased with her for winning the back crawl.

They had left the relay race until last; six swimmers in either team and under the eye of the judges they drew for their places – slips of folded paper from a plastic bowl – and Rob was second and Val third. The race was free-style, and the cheers started as soon as the first two competitors hit the water.

'If you swim like you did before, you'll win it on your own,' Rob said as they stood watching.

'I've changed my mind,' Val said, 'I'm going to do front crawl.'

'Oh?' He glanced at her, surprised.

'Why not? It's a fast stroke.'

'Yes, I know . . .'

The two number ones had turned and were heading back across the pool in a whirl of spray. Rob began to brace himself, ready to touch the outstretched hand before plunging in. The cheers and shrieks increased, Val wished him good luck and then he was away, about three seconds ahead of his rival. Val started cheering too; jigging up and down and shouting: *'Come on, Rob!'* The rest of the team took up the cry, and school was all that mattered; school was all that was real and good and worth belonging to.

She began preparing for the racing dive even before he had reached the far end of the pool; crouching down with her feet braced, but with her eyes fixed on the dark bob of hair in the distance, not shouting now because she wanted to conserve all her energy. He turned, and began bouncing towards her in a rapid breast stroke, his shoulders lifting out of the water and dropping back again, his mouth opening in a wide O as he gulped in air.

He had lengthened the gap from a couple of seconds to about fifteen, and fresh shrieks of applause broke out as he and Val touched fingers and she plunged in.

She seemed to shoot through the water like a

projectile, the side of her face nestled deep in a pillow of flying spray and the ear that was uppermost was catching the wild echoing voices from her teammates and her school friends – all of them urging her on, faster and faster; all of them calling her name 'Val – Val!' with a loving rapture that drew the last ounce of strength from her.

Then it happened. As she gulped a breath she forgot the self-imposed rule of not looking up at the spectators' gallery, and her water-blurred eye caught and registered the shock of someone with bright red curly hair sitting in the front row. It was Mud.

She faltered. Lost the rhythmic co-ordination of arms and legs and breath and was barely conscious of switching from front crawl to breast stroke so that she could keep her gaze fixed on that bright bunch of merry red curls. The shrieks of applause began to turn to shrieks of horror, but she was unaware of that too; instantly she had changed from a high-powered, fiercely competitive machine into something governed by blind and primitive instinct. Her destination was no longer the end of the pool and back again, it was the person up there in the gallery. The screams of warning bubbled in her ears unheeded, and swimming diagonally it was only a matter of seconds before she crashed into the flailing limbs of her opponent.

They both sank. Then rose, disentangling, to the surface and the boy from the other school spat water and hatred at Val and called her a stupid bitch. The words, bawled in a voice cracking with fury, rose to a high shriek that everyone heard; some of them laughed, but from Val's school came a long low wail of agony as the presiding judge blew his whistle and ordered the two competitors from the water. The relay race was declared cancelled.

'What happened – what happened?'

'Were you ill? Were you ill?'

Funny how they all seemed to repeat everything, as if asking once wasn't enough.

'Did you get cramp? Was it cramp?'

But she shoved them all aside, all of them, whoever they were, then picked up her towel and walked off. A buzz of speculation and a few jeers followed her and just before leaving the poolside she looked up at the gallery again and it wasn't Mud after all. It was a woman with red curly hair all right, but she was fat and ugly and eating a banana.

There was no one else in the changing rooms. Stony-faced she peeled off her costume, dried herself and put on her clothes. Her hair was still wet and she combed it behind her ears. She felt cold, teeth-chatteringly cold, and she hated and loathed everyone and every single thing in the whole of the universe.

'Mind if I walk with you?'

'Please yourself.'

'Where are we going?'

'I'm going to my sister's? You can go where you like.'

Val had left the sports complex and gone past the

school to the end of the road when Rob caught up with her. His hair was still wet too, and he smelt of chlorine.

They walked in silence, Val slouching along with her swimming things in a carrier bag. They reached the main road, and the pavements were crowded with Saturday afternoon shoppers and noisy with the sound of traffic.

'I've got a better idea,' Rob said. 'I've just had my pigeon money, so I'll buy you some tea.'

'No, thanks.'

'Oh, come on, Val –'

'I *don't want* any –'

'Do as you're told and stop being so daft –'

He shoved her hard with his shoulder and she found herself stumbling through the open doorway of a snack bar. Her fury burst into flame.

'How dare you, Rob Lacey! Just you stop bossing me around!'

'Now, now, you two,' said the man who was wiping down the counter. 'What'll it be – tea or coffee?'

'Neither,' said Val.

'Two teas, please,' said Rob. 'With milk and sugar.'

'Got some nice Eccles cakes,' the man said. 'Fresh in this morning.'

'And two Eccles cakes.' Rob half-guided and half-pushed Val on to a bench seat at a vacant table. He sat down next to her, trapping her against the wall.

'It's no use, you won't get me to eat or drink anything.'

He didn't reply, and they sat in silence as the man poured the tea from an urn, slapped the cups on to two saucers and shuffled across with them. He went back for the Eccles cakes.

'Shall I pay now?' Rob asked, and produced a carefully folded five-pound note from the back of his jeans. 'I'm sorry I've nothing smaller,' he said politely.

He seemed very adult; very kindly and mature, and when he touched her bare forearm and said: 'Come on, now, drink up, there's a good girl,' the anger drained away and left a deep aching misery in its place.

'What's your pigeon money?' she asked gruffly.

'An old bloke near us breeds racing pigeons. I help him clean them out when I get home from school.'

'Oh.' The tea looked golden and inviting. Tentatively she stirred it with the teaspoon.

'I got cramp once when I was swimming,' Rob said. 'I really thought I was going to drown.'

'It wasn't cramp with me.'

He didn't say anything, didn't pry, but the sense of kindness that came from him made her want to weep. She felt the tears stinging, but blinked them back and then took a mouthful of tea.

'I just went crooked because I started thinking about something else.'

'Loss of concentration,' Rob said. 'Not to worry, it can easily happen.'

'But I let everybody down. They had to cancel it because of me, and then when that boy called me – called me a –' She tried to check her tears but they overflowed. She groped unsuccessfully for a hand-kerchief.

'He was just a yob. Not worth crying about –'

'I've never been called that word before.' Val was now crying hard. She groped under the table for the carrier bag and wiped her eyes on her rolled-up towel. 'It was all so happy and nice and I was swimming well and I knew that everyone was pleased and that I was going to do everything right for once . . . I so wanted our school to win because school's all I really care about . . .'

'Look,' Rob said, 'eat your Eccles cake –'

'I think families are a waste of time and I'm going to live with my sister – she thinks the same thing – and I honestly don't care if I don't see either of my parents again. I just want to be on my *own* –'

'But you won't be on your own if you're living with your sister, will you?' Rob said.

'You don't know my sister. Her body might be there but her mind isn't.'

'You mean she's mentally retarded?'

'No – just the opposite. She's the only person I know who's got it all worked out. She just wants to be *her*, and not get messed about by other people, because they're selfish and stupid and don't care how much they hurt people –' She crammed a hunk of Eccles cake into her mouth, then her sobs burst out again and she choked violently.

'Take a drink of tea –' He thumped her on the back.

She did so, slopping some of it in the saucer.

'That's better. Now calm down and listen. You're not going to go and live with your sister, because it's running away. Something's gone wrong and you don't have to tell me what it is unless you want to – but it's no use running away. Opting out's feeble, Val.' He took her hand and held it, and although she wanted to wrench it away, she didn't.

'Yes, but you don't know –'

'I know I don't know. And I'm not asking. But whatever's wrong you've got to fight back. You've got to grit your teeth and go on –'

'One thing I won't go on doing, and that's swimming –' She dried her eyes on the towel again.

'Oh yes, you will – that's exactly what I mean. You've got to forget about what happened in the relay race –'

'They had to cancel it because of me –'

'Well, okay, there'll be another one next year. It's not the end of the world, is it?'

'It isn't just that. I mean, it's bad enough letting everybody down in front of everybody else, and being laughed at and being hated because you're a bungling idiot, but that's not all of it. I've got other troubles as well – deep, awful ones, and all this time I've been trying to go on being loyal and sensible and practical and all the things I'm really not – but I just can't any longer –'

Sitting there side by side he turned his head to look at her; instinctively she turned her own, and he leaned across and kissed her. A grave, dry little kiss full on the mouth.

99

'Well –'

'Sorry,' he said. 'If you've finished your tea, shall we go?'

Outside, the sun was still hot, although the shoppers were diminishing. The street had a jaded, exhausted look.

'Promise you won't go and live with your sister,' he said. 'Promise you'll go home and do everything the way you did before.'

'But you don't know what way I was doing things, before.'

'No. But I'm sure it was right.'

He walked with her to the bus stop. 'And will you come swimming at the lake tomorrow afternoon?'

'I don't ever want to go swimming again.'

'Yes, you do. One bad experience doesn't put people off doing nice things for the rest of their lives.'

'In any case, I don't think I can get away,' she said. Then added defiantly: 'I mean, whether I'm at home or with my sister.'

'I'll be there anyway,' Rob said. 'Around three.'

He flicked his hand in a quick goodbye gesture and walked away.

The first bus that came was not the one that led to home, but she climbed aboard and sat inside thinking that it was all very well for Rob Lacey to boss her about when he had no idea of the real state of things. He had no more right to tell her to go home than he had to tell her to go swimming.

She got off the bus at the end of Theo's road and

walked, swinging her carrier bag, to the sad, decaying house where the squatters lived.

She climbed the stairs and banged on Theo's door, but there was no reply. She turned the handle and walked in, and although its furnishings had been somewhat spartan on the occasion of her first visit, now the room was totally empty save for a small heap of miscellaneous rubbish in the fireplace.

Val stood considering the place in silence for a minute or two, then slowly walked downstairs again. She met a young West Indian in the hall and asked him if he knew where Theo was.

'The guy on the top floor?'

'My sister . . .'

'The guy with the crazy hair? She's gone, man.'

'Oh no . . . When?'

The West Indian propped himself against the broken banister and assumed the expression of someone desperately scouring their memory.

'Can't rightly say. Last week. Yesterday. One day's pretty like another.'

'And you don't know *where* she's gone, either?'

'If she don't tell and I don't ask, then I guess there's a good chance I don't.'

'No, I s'pose not. Well, thank you . . .'

'Any time, man,' said the West Indian, and slid gracefully away.

When Val reached home she found Father and Mrs Forrest sitting in the garden in deckchairs. Mrs Forrest was knitting a long length of something pink and Father was reading a book, and the atmosphere of deep peacefulness made them seem like an old, happily married couple.

Without saying anything Val hung out her damp swimming things and went up to her bedroom and closed the door.

# CHAPTER SEVEN

But she honestly couldn't get over Rob Lacey kissing her like that.

Lots of the other girls had boyfriends and talked about kissing and all that, but Val had never joined in; partly because she had never really wanted to, and partly because no one had invited her to.

She liked Rob quite a lot, and a few weeks ago would probably not have been averse to trying him out in the role of boyfriend – to start with, it would have been one in the eye for Alice, who was very sniffy about romance – but now, things were different.

Now she no longer believed in loving people. People you thought were safe as houses let you down, and she wasn't going to start loving Rob (in *any* sort of way), because sooner or later he'd find someone else he liked better. And she certainly wasn't going to let him kiss her again. Kissing was horrible. The thought of Mud kissing Bill Bridge and Father kissing Mrs Forrest made her feel ill, and she vowed that when she grew up, a dog like Sheepshanks would provide all the companionship necessary.

In the meantime, school term had ended and the

prospect of eight weeks' holiday at home yawned drearily ahead. Eight weeks of cooking and making beds and seeing to things – and having to cope with the twins as well during Mrs Forrest's two-week trip to Majorca.

It was a wonder that Father hadn't announced that he was going with her ('You'll be able to manage, won't you, Val? Here's some money – take the boys to the zoo for the day, they'd like that . . .''. But he hadn't said anything. He hadn't said much about anything at all since the night of the supper party; just mooched about at home looking miserable, but once when Val cut her finger slicing cucumber for a salad, he had held it under the cold tap, then dried it and put a plaster on it with such tenderness, and had looked at her as if he was longing to say something loving and special. But he had remained silent, and so had she, except for thanking him.

And so the gap between them all grew wider and wider, and to go off and live the kind of life that Theo did seemed the only sensible thing to do. She wished she knew where Theo was now, because she sensed that she was the only person she could talk to who would understand.

The next day was Sunday, and she spent most of the morning tidying her bedroom. Really tidying it, as if she were planning to leave very soon. Clothes she had grown out of she packed in a cardboard box, and then sat on the floor methodically tearing up a stack of old school exercise books and stuffing the bits into a plastic bag. In a way, it was like saying goodbye to herself.

Then Bardo came in, picked up a volume of intermediate geometry and said: 'Please can I have this?'

'What for?'

'Well, I'm starting school in September and I'll need some books, won't I?'

'Yes, but not that sort.'

'What's wrong with this sort?' He clutched it to his bosom.

'It's too old.'

'I don't mind old books providing the pages aren't falling out.'

'I didn't mean old in that sense,' Val said wearily. 'I mean it's too old for *you*. You won't be starting with books like that, you'll have little easy ones and work your way up to the hard ones.'

Bardo stared at her in silence for a moment, then said: 'I'm afraid I don't understand you. Books are books, so far as I'm concerned.'

How easy everything was when you were the twins' age. Black-and-white was black-and-white, and books were books until you learned how to read.

'Okay, have it your way,' she said. 'I won't be needing it any more.'

She sat on the floor with her knees drawn up under her chin and thought goodbye, goodbye, I'm leaving all this behind. I've decided I'm not going back to school. They can't make me. They couldn't make Theo and they won't be able to make me. I'll see them through the holidays but that's all. That's the end, goodbye.

But, feeling the way she did, it needed a superhuman willpower even to stay at home all day during that Sunday. She cooked lunch, washed the dishes, and at half past two said to Father: 'Will you take care of the boys this afternoon? I've got to go out.'

'Got to?' Father said mildly. 'Whose orders?'

'I'd arranged to meet a friend,' Val said, and felt her cheeks turn pink.

'Mrs Forrest may be popping in later,' Father said. 'So I expect we'll be all right.'

Up until that moment she would have changed her mind if he had asked her to. If he'd said that he'd been looking forward to her company that afternoon she would have stayed at home and done her best to make things lively and interesting the way Mud used to. But with Mrs Forrest to play understudy, there was no need.

So although she had decided never to go swimming again and that she didn't really like Rob Lacey after all, she packed her towel and costume and set off on her bicycle to Beauchamp Park.

He was already there when she arrived; sitting under a tree in his swimming trunks and chewing a blade of grass. She went behind the same tree she always used, and when the zip on her jeans stuck halfway down with a bit of her briefs caught in its teeth, she struggled out of both garments simultaneously, suddenly panic-stricken in case Rob turned round, saw the predicament she was in and came over to help.

But he didn't. He remained sitting there with his

back to her, and it crossed her mind that perhaps he didn't really like her either.

'Hello, Val.'

'Uh-huh.'

'I think the water'll be very warm.'

'Have you been in already?'

'No, I waited for you.'

They stood side by side on the lichened paving. The sleepy murmur of wood pigeons was the only sound and Val stared across the lake to the sad, shuttered old house.

'I don't like it here any more,' she said. 'I'm going.'

'Have a swim first. It's a waste to come all this way for nothing.'

'I don't want to.'

The water had a black, oily look that reflected the sky and the trees, and the bulrushes over on the far side stood like a forest of cruel dark swords. Shivering, she took a step backwards.

If he pushes me in I'll drown, she thought. I don't want to swim. I can't swim – I've forgotten how . . . The shame of the gala nibbled at her mind as if it would never never go away.

But he didn't push her in. He just dived neatly and cleanly into the lake and swam away from her towards the big broken fountain in the centre. A moorhen fled for cover with a wild shriek of alarm.

Rob turned towards her, treading water. 'Just come in for a few minutes. Swim over to the fountain and back and then we'll both go home.'

Still she hung back, wretched with nerves. Out of all the muck-ups she had made in her life, the swimming gala muck-up had been the most resoundingly awful. And certainly the most public. Even now the memory of the final race made her want to cry out with the burning pain of it. She had let them all down. Ruined the whole grand finale, and all because she thought she'd seen someone she knew. Someone she *once* knew . . .

Val closed her eyes, and when she opened them again Rob was still over by the fountain, treading water and smiling at her with his hair streaked down flat and shining.

Taking a deep breath she made herself dive in and swim towards him.

She didn't sink, and she hadn't forgotten how. Like ointment soothing a sore place, the feel of the water seemed to bring a strange peace. Even a hint of the old happiness.

She reached Rob's side, and was grateful when he didn't say things like *There you are! I told you you could!* . . . In fact he didn't say anything at all, but just swam quietly and lazily in and out of the reflections of sky criss-crossed with the branches of trees. It occurred to Val that he wasn't challenging her to a race because of what happened at the gala. Very cautiously, she started liking him again.

They swam, climbed out and dived in again for a long while, and it was one of those long, motionless summer afternoons when even the sun seemed to stay fixed in one spot about the treetops, and nightfall seemed as remote as the idea of Christmas.

'We ought to be going soon,' Rob said.

'Ten more minutes.' Now that she had overcome the dread of swimming, she didn't want to stop.

So they went on as before, breasting the placid water side by side, listening to the quiet pluck-pluck-pluck of the moorhen and gazing across the bulrushes to the old house sitting in the ruins of a once beautiful garden.

'I wouldn't mind living in a place like that,' Val said. 'All on my own.'

'You'd be a bit lonely.'

'I'd be able to live my own life, though, wouldn't I?'

'Don't think that'd be much consolation after the first couple of weeks. No one to argue with, for instance.'

'I don't ever argue. It's boring.'

'Perhaps that's the trouble.' Rob gave her a side-long look as they reached the remains of the fountain. 'If you argued more, you wouldn't be so fed up with whatever it is.'

'I'm getting fed up with you, Rob Lacey,' Val said, but only jokingly.

He grinned at her, and she turned on her back and kicked up a blinding mountain of water in front of him and it was like going back to the beginning of their friendship; before Mud had left home, and before the gala.

Then Rob climbed out and stood poised on the broken edge of the fountain for a moment before diving in again. And he didn't come up. The rings widened on the water but he didn't break surface. The lake settled back into its dark mirror-like calm and there was still no Rob. Just a small string of bubbles lying for a moment like little silver pearls before bursting to nothingness.

Treading water she stared at the place where she had last seen him, then abruptly plunged with down-pointing arms and kicking legs.

It was difficult to see much because of the fine particles of mud that floated between the long fronds of water weed, but she was able to make out a dark blur lying motionless below her. She grabbed at it, and Rob's body slithered in her grasp. His head was against something cold and hard and his left ankle was caught in a tangle of rubbery weed.

She put her arms round him, and pulled. Then let go and wrenched desperately at the clinging green fingers that held him. She tore his foot free, and with bursting lungs shot with him to the surface.

His eyes were closed, and the water washed at the blood coming from a gash on his forehead. Gulping in air she seized a handful of his thick slippery hair then turned on her side and began to stroke for the shore.

He was unbelievably heavy. Grimly she fixed her gaze on the nearest stone dolphin and swam towards it, striving to regulate her breathing and to gain maximum benefit from each kick of her legs, each thrust of her one free arm, but progress seemed bitterly slow. Her heart was pounding more and more, and she didn't know whether it was with exertion or panic. Probably both. She stopped staring at the dolphin for a moment and raked the surrounding trees and bushes for any sign of another human presence. She had no strength to call for help, but it didn't matter, because there was nobody. Nothing. Even the moorhen seemed to have disappeared.

And then, even when she reached the edge of the lake there was the problem of how to get Rob out of the water. She couldn't pull him out by his hair. Panting, she hauled herself on to the rim and then tugged at his shoulders. She got his arms out and lying on the warm stone, his head turned to one side. Then she got back into the water and somehow shunted the rest of him out.

It took a long, long while, and when finally he lay spreadeagled in the golden sunshine he looked as if he were dead.

She burst into tears, then. And at the same moment remembered about artificial respiration.

She didn't know how to do it. At school they wouldn't be taught life-saving until next year. With the tears running down her cheeks she gave him a hard and exasperated thump between the shoulder-blades, and Rob's whole body seemed to heave in one huge and painful intake of breath that ended in a violent spasm of choking.

She thumped him again and the water poured out of his mouth and down his nose. He groaned, and was sick, but she went on thumping him because it seemed to be helping, and anyway she didn't know what else to do.

He groaned again, and managed to roll over on to his back. His eyes opened. He looked at her wonderingly.

'You always seem to be crying these days.'

'If I am, it's not because of you,' Val said roughly.

'My head hurts . . .'

'You must have cut it when you dived off the fountain.'

'When?'

'Just now.'

'I don't remember . . .'

He tried to sit up, got so far and then collapsed in a faint. She caught the back of his head in her hands just before it met the stone paving. She laid it down gently, and the blood was still oozing from the cut over his right eye. She fetched the handkerchief from her jeans pocket, dipped it in the lake, folded it into a compress and laid it over the wound. She didn't know what else to do, so sat with her knees drawn up under her chin and watched him. She felt that she would never be so silently close to any other person as she was to him just then.

He regained consciousness, and began to shiver violently. As if in sympathy, she found herself doing the same. Her limbs shook and her teeth chattered. She ran for their towels, laid Rob's over him, but dazedly he sat up and began to dry himself.

'Are you all right now?'

'Think so. What happened?'

'You fainted.'

'When?' The improvised compress fell off the cut and he stared at the blood on it uncomprehendingly.

'I told you. You dived, and must have hit your head. I think it was on the remains of the fountain lying on the bottom. Then your foot got caught in the weeds . . . but you're all right now, aren't you?'

'Yes.' He gave her a painful little smile. 'I just feel so cold.'

'You'd better get dressed. Come on, I'll help you.'

He stood up, wavering slightly, as she towelled his hair, dried his back and arms and then gruffly ordered him to take his swimming trunks off. He did so, with his back to her, and she went to fetch his clothes and stood supporting his arm as he struggled into them. Then she rinsed out the handkerchief, refolded it and clamped it back on his forehead.

'Do you feel up to cycling home?'

'Yes. I'll be okay.'

'You'll have to ride with one hand and hold the handkerchief with the other.'

'Yes . . .'

'Shall I come with you?'

'No. I'm all right.'

'But if you'll just wait till I've got changed . . .'

'No, I want to go now . . .'

They went over to the two bicycles and she watched dubiously as he hauled himself on to the saddle.

'Wait, Rob,' she said. 'You can't go on your own –'

'Leave me,' he said. 'I'm quite all right.'

He rode off down the bumpy path, and to prove that he was all right, turned round and waved. He almost fell off.

Still shivering, Val stripped off her own wet costume, tore her briefs from the zip of her jeans and hurried clammily into her clothes. She set off with the intention of catching him up, then changed her mind.

If Rob Lacey could do without her, she could do without him. She didn't need him or anyone else.

Although she was tired, she didn't hurry home. There was nothing to hurry home for.

I'm the odd one out, she thought. Father's got Mrs Forrest, the twins have got each other, and Theo doesn't want anybody. Then she remembered that she didn't want anybody either, and felt a bit better.

Shoving her bicycle through the open back garden gate she left it propped against the wall and then went up to the house. It was empty, the key to the kitchen door under the flowerpot they always used as a hiding place.

She went indoors. Everywhere looked reasonably tidy, but it wasn't homely any more. There were no bunches of flowers in vases and the rooms smelt stale because no one ever remembered to open the windows now.

She went upstairs to her bedroom and flung herself on the bed, but whenever she closed her eyes she kept seeing the cut on Rob's forehead welling blood. She wondered if he had got home all right,

114

then told herself that if he hadn't it was his own fault. After all, she had offered to go with him . . .

She got off the bed and rambled downstairs again. The kitchen had the same tidy, unloved look as everywhere else; two cups and saucers (Father's and Mrs Forrest's) standing upside down to dry on the sink unit, two pairs of red canvas shoes belonging to the twins standing to attention side by side. Even poor old Sheepshanks' basket had its blanket neatly folded . . .

Sheepshanks. She looked round. Where was he?

She called his name as she went through to the hall and looked through the open doorways. Sometimes he liked to sleep on the old sofa in Father's study, but he wasn't there now.

'Sheepshanks . . . Sheepie – where are you?'

No sign. No sounds. She went out into the garden, and then she remembered that the gate had been open when she arrived back. She ran to it, and peered up the alleyway that ran between the backs of the houses, and of course he wasn't there. The gate had probably been open for ages and he could be miles away by now.

But she had to do something. Quickly. So, dashing back to the house, she relocked the door and went out through the alleyway, calling his name and peering through the gates of the other houses.

She came out into the street and stood looking first one way and then the other, wondering which direction to take. A very old man walking along with a pekinese on a lead prompted her to say: 'Excuse

115

me, but have you seen a big dog running loose? He's sort of brown and black with –'

'This dog's father was a champion,' the old man said, pausing to admire his pekinese. 'Won all the top prizes in his class at Crufts.'

'Yes,' Val said, 'it's beautiful. But our dog's only a mongrel, and he must have got out by accident –'

'It's a her,' the old man said. 'Not an it. Animals have as much right to be called hims and hers as the human race. More so, if you ask me.'

'Yes,' Val said, dashing on. 'Thank you very much.'

'You humans are all the same,' he shouted after her. 'Arrogant, haughty, supercilious –'

'You're a human being too!' Val shouted back. 'Super-silly you, never mind super-silly us!'

She came to the main road, and remembered that if anyone ever took Sheepshanks out shopping, his favourite port of call was the butcher's. Ignoring the traffic lights she hurried across to the opposite side, and of course the butcher's shop – like all the others – was closed. She stood motionless, trying to regain her breath and staring into the window with its empty white trays and borders of plastic parsley, and she didn't know where to go or what to do next.

She was still tired – in fact, more tired than ever now – and it was only the conviction that Sheepshanks was the one person she could love and trust that kept her going. So she trailed up one street and down the next, calling his name and stopping every now and then to ask passers-by if they had seen a large mongrel dog, sort of black and brown, running

116

along looking lost and worried, which he would be by now . . .

But none of them had. One of them froze her blood by saying that a dog had been run over that afternoon outside the public library, and another one told her that the lady-next-door's spaniel had been stolen and sold to a laboratory for experimental purposes, only that was three months ago . . . then finally a sensible-looking woman in bifocals asked whether she had inquired at the police station.

And of course she hadn't.

The sky had turned to evening purple and the street lights were glinting when she entered the big double doors and the desk sergeant asked her to take a seat while telephones kept ringing and people kept coming in and out. She had no idea that police stations were so busy, particularly on Sundays.

So she sat reading a notice about what to do if she found a Colorado beetle until at last the sergeant said: 'Right now, miss, what can I do for you?'

'I've called to see if you've found our dog,' Val said politely but wearily. She went over to him. 'He's lost.'

'Name?' The sergeant took up a ballpoint pen.

'Sheepshanks.'

'And your address, Miss Sheepshanks?'

'Oh no – I'm Valeria Hope. It's our dog that's –'

'Your address, Miss Hope?'

'Twenty-four Elphinstone Road.'

He asked a lot of other things, such as her telephone number, her age, and whether she lived with her parents. He seemed far more interested in her than in Sheepshanks.

117

'Now then' he said finally. 'What is it you've lost?'

'A dog,' Val said.

'Can you furnish a description?' He waited, pen poised, and Val thought I've never heard of people furnishing descriptions; only things like houses.

'Yes,' she said. 'He's quite big, with a rough, shortish sort of coat, and he's brown and black. Well, it's mostly brown but he's got sort of little black eyebrows and his ears are black – at least, one's more black than the other – and his tail's fairly long with a bit of a curl in it – not so much of a curl, on second thoughts, as a bend. I mean, it curls when he's pleased and sags down when he isn't, but most of the time it's in what you'd call a bend.'

The sergeant listened patiently, then said: 'Was the animal wearing a collar?'

'Oh no, he only wears his collar when he goes out for walks,' Val said. And then faltered. Her face turned fiery red and she began to back away when she realized that that was precisely where Sheepshanks might be. Out for a walk with Father and the twins. Anyone with a grain of sense would have looked for his collar and lead before dashing out on a wild-goose chase.

'I think that's all I can tell you,' she mumbled. 'I mean, if you do hear anything we'd be very glad if you could . . .' she continued to back away, 'let . . . us . . . know . . .'

Of course that was where Sheepshanks was; up on the common with Father and the boys. Why oh why hadn't she stopped to add two and two together? Why hadn't she even bothered to wonder where Father and the twins had gone? It could only prove beyond any lingering doubt that she no longer cared two straws for any of them.

It also proved that she had just made another monumental muck of things.

# CHAPTER EIGHT

'Thank you very much,' Val said from over by the door. 'I'm sorry to have wasted your time . . .'

'Just a minute, miss,' the sergeant said. 'We haven't quite finished, have we?'

Very reluctantly Val crept back again. 'I've suddenly thought that there's just a chance that he might have . . .'

'What time did the dog in question go missing?'

'I'm not sure. Some time this afternoon. That is, if he –'

'If he what, miss?' The sergeant was now studying her with frank suspicion.

'If he got out of his own accord or if he – if by any chance – and it's only a sort of idea, if he got taken out *by* somebody –'

'Stolen, you mean?'

It wasn't what she meant. But she nodded, all the same.

The sergeant laid down his pen and then folded his arms on top of the desk. He subjected Val to another long stare which deepened the colour in her cheeks from peony to beetroot.

'Now then, miss,' he said. 'I've got precisely four minutes to spare and I'm going to spend it in telling

you exactly what I think about dogs and their owners. We'll take dogs first. Now, the dog is an animal
closely related to the wolf; in other words, it is a
pack animal. Which means that it never makes a
decision without first having a committee meeting.
Sometimes as a result of which it takes the right
decision, but more often the wrong one, like worrying sheep, or –'

'Chasing cats?'

'Cats,' said the sergeant coldly, 'are of even less
account than dogs, so we'll forget about them. But
returning to the aforesaid species, you can lump the
whole lot together – watch dogs, gun dogs, lap dogs
– dogs with bends in their tails, dogs without bends
in their tails, dogs without any tails at all, and you
can put them all down under one heading. Vermin.
They're all, without any possible exception, dirty,
untrustworthy, immoral, and thick. Thick as your
ankle. Thick as a butterbean stew.'

'Our dog isn't like that –' Val protested.

'Now we come to humans,' the sergeant continued,
quelling her with a look. 'Homo sapiens, and the
aforesaid owner of the aforesaid dog. And if dogs
are thick, the sheer thickness of the average proud
doggy-owner passeth all understanding. We've had
dog-owners in here who refuse all responsibility
when their Fido bites somebody else's baby – some
nice quiet little baby lying in its pram minding its
own business – Fido was only looking at it, they say,
and his teeth slipped. We've had people in here
whose dogs have savaged old ladies, torn postmen
limb from limb, mutilated little children, and the

owners always say oh, but it wasn't his fault! He's not well, or he's psychologically disturbed, or else he's ate something that's disagreed with him. Most likely what he's ate was the leg off of the woman next door –'

The sergeant's rage seemed to be increasing. His face was now almost as red as Val's.

'I'm very sorry,' she whispered, without knowing what she was supposed to be sorry for.

'But the worst thing of all about dog-owners is their sheer inefficiency. Their complete inability to control the animal in question. Now take yourself, miss; a typical dog-owner in the form of a spoilt young girl whose Mammy and Daddy buys her every mortal thing she wants. I want a dog, she says, so all right, here you are, they say to her, here's a nice dog for you with a bend in its tail. And I bet your parents wait on you hand and foot, give you everything you want, including your own video and word-processor, I shouldn't be surprised –'

'It's not like that,' Val said, the wicked unfairness of his words reducing her voice to a croak. 'And I'm going now.'

She went back to the door.

'Come back,' ordered the sergeant. 'Or don't you want your dog after all?'

Her jaw sagged. 'You mean – he's here?'

'Could answer to the same description. You'd better come and make an identification.'

He led her through a door and down a long stone corridor and out into a yard where police cars were parked. Over in a corner was a row of wire cages

122

and in one of them, in an attitude of utter dejection, lay Sheepshanks.

'*Sheepshanks!*'

He leaped when he heard her voice, and scrabbled at the wire. He barked a joyous greeting.

'Is that him?'

'Yes,' Val said, choked with relief. 'That's him.'

The sergeant disappeared for a moment and came back with a length of rope. He made a noose in one end, went into the cage and slipped it over Sheepshanks' head. The other end he gave to Val.

'There you are,' he said, and patted her shoulder. 'Now be a good kid and take care of him.'

He walked away, and in the middle of all the relief and the gladness it occurred to Val that perhaps he didn't mind dogs (or their owners) quite as much as he said he did.

It was a long walk back from the police station, and to begin with, her progress was impeded by Sheepshanks jumping up at her; but after a while he settled down and trotted quietly by her side.

He looked awful with a rope round his neck instead of a collar and lead, but at least it proved one thing; he *had* been lost, and she *had* done the right thing by dashing out to look for him. She wished now that she'd had the courage to stick up for herself a bit more in the police station – her indignation still simmered at the memory of the sergeant calling her a spoilt young girl whose parents waited on her hand and foot. If only he knew the truth of it.

They left the main street and turned the corner into Elphinstone Road. Val's legs were aching, and she spoke impatiently to Sheepshanks when he suddenly halted and stood in front of her with his ears pricked.

'Come *on* –' she said, but he remained standing there, bristling slightly.

What happened next seemed to happen at lightning speed, and she had received no more than a shadowy impression of someone standing motionless by the alleyway when Sheepshanks gave an abrupt lurch forward. Unprepared, and with the rope wound round her hand, Val was jerked along behind him. She stumbled, almost recovered her balance, then sprawled heavily. Her chin hit the pavement and her teeth rattled. The rope unwound from her hand and when the stars stopped dancing in front of her eyes she slowly raised her head and propped her aching jaw on her hand.

She couldn't sit up. Couldn't do anything but remain sprawled dazedly on the quiet evening pavement while she watched Sheepshanks and tried to work out what was going on. Never, never had she seen him behave like this before.

Stopping in mid-lurch with one front paw raised he gave a couple of sharp barks – barks with a question mark at the end of them. Then suddenly he screamed – a terrible high primitive scream and galloped towards the human figure still standing in the shadows. He leaped at it, bounding like a huge and ungainly rubber ball, and still Val couldn't find the strength to move.

124

Then grunting with exertion Sheepshanks sped back to her in what the family had always called his Funny Run; his behind tucked in, front legs splaying sideways and eyes mad as he scuttled rapidly along with the rope flying out behind him. Reaching Val he licked her face, seized a lump of her hair in his hot panting mouth, let it go again, then scuttled back to the person who was still standing by the entrance to the alleyway. He barked and whined and sobbed and flung himself again and again at whoever it was, and the pain in Val's jaw was just beginning to ease when Mud stepped out of the shadows, grasped Sheepshanks' rope and walked slowly towards her.

'Val, dear,' she said, 'do get up, or you'll get trodden on.'

Val got up, very slowly. She stood rubbing her jaw and looking at Mud and she didn't know what to say. In the end she just said: 'Hello.'

'I can't get in,' Mud said. 'I didn't take my own latchkey and the back door key isn't under the flowerpot.'

'Yes, it is,' Val said. 'I know it is because I put it there.'

In all the strangeness and confusion of suddenly seeing Mud again it was a great help to be able to concentrate on everyday objects like door keys. 'I put it there before I went off to look for Sheepshanks, who got out by accident.'

'How strange,' said Mud. 'It's not there now.'

They walked down the alleyway together, Sheepshanks still pausing every now and then to scrabble

125

fondly at Mud. Without saying anything they went through the garden gate, walked up the path to the house, and when Mud lifted the flowerpot there was no key beneath it.

'See?'

'Yes,' said Val, 'I see.' And in the constrained little silence which ensued, she slid her hand into her jeans pocket and of course there it was. The back door key.

She opened the door, and halfway over the threshold turned to look at Mud, and a combination of weariness and shock made her speak sharply.

'D'you want to come in?'

'Yes, please,' Mud said.

'Have you come back to stay?'

'Yes.'

Suppressing an Alice-type *Hmm*, Val walked in ahead of her. Sheepshanks broke into his Funny Run again, hauled the neatly folded blanket from his basket and dragged it over towards Mud.

'I don't want it, you silly old dog.'

'He's pleased to see you,' Val said, still fairly sharp.

'Are you, too?'

They sat down opposite one another at the big kitchen table.

'I don't know,' Val said. 'I suppose I would be if I didn't know that everything's different now.'

'How's it different?'

Indignation suddenly brought Val close to tears. 'It's all different in every single possible way! You and Father don't love each other any more – you've

both got someone else and you don't care about us –
you only care about yourselves like a lot of other
parents, including Janice Brewer's . . . she's had to go
and live with her auntie, who she really hates, and it
means she can't come to our school any more or see
any of her friends and it's all because her parents are
selfish and rotten and getting divorced –'

'What makes you think I want to get divorced?'
Mud asked in a quiet little voice.

Val dragged her fist across her eyes. 'So that you
can get married to Bill Bridge.'

'So that I can – *what*?' Mud's voice was now a
hoarse whisper.

'And so that Father can marry Mrs Forrest. She
comes here nearly every day –'

'I know she does –'

'How d'you know she does?'

'I know,' Mud said tiredly, 'because I've been
living with her sister Lilian. She writes poetry.'

'*Who?*'

'Mrs Forrest's sister. You've got it all wrong, Val.
I didn't go away with Bill Bridge – *him*, for heaven's
sake! – I went away because I wanted to work.'

'Work? What at?'

'At sculpture, of course.'

'If that's the case, why couldn't you work at it
here?' It was as if Val didn't want to believe her;
didn't want to have her back again.

'Because,' Mud said, with a hint of her old impa-
tience, 'I got fed up with always having to put myself
second to all the rest of you. It's all right for wives
and mothers to do what they want to do *when*

127

they've finished running round after their families. Sometimes they want to be free to do things first thing in the morning while they're still feeling fresh and energetic, and *not* after they've made the beds and swept and dusted and shopped and cooked and seen to the washing. They get fed up with looking after people who ought to be quite capable of looking after themselves — husbands who can't find their shoes, daughters who can't be bothered to come home in time for meals — and they get absolutely sick and tired of being patronized. Yes, dear, that's a very nice piece of sculpture but where's my clean shirt? Yes, Mud, I think you're very clever but what's for supper? I may not bother to be home in time, but I like to know all the same . . .'

Val opened her mouth to say something, thought better of it, so closed it again.

'And that's when they start dreaming about a little place of their own. A little private room where they can do what they want to do all day long with nobody coming to interfere or nag them about things.'

'But what about Bill Bridge?' Val said finally. 'I mean, even if you weren't —'

'He nagged too,' Mud said. 'He seemed to think that I showed possible signs of talent for sculpture, but he wouldn't leave me alone. I wanted him to teach me, but not to take me over. He kept trying to make me copy other people when all I wanted was help in learning how to express myself. So I left his class although he tried to persuade me not to — he even called round here one evening —'

128

'Yes,' Val said. 'I remember.'

'Flattering in a way, I suppose, but I know I did the right thing by striking out on my own. And when I bumped into Mary Forrest for the first time in years – I didn't even know her husband had died – and I told her that I'd love to have somewhere of my own to work in, she said that Lilian had a big attic at the top of her house that she didn't use, so we planned it all between the three of us and then we dressed ourselves up one evening and went out to supper to celebrate.'

Mud propped her chin on her hand and looked dreamy. 'It was a beautiful attic. No furniture, no curtains, just a camp bed and lots of lovely uncluttered space and nobody to interrupt. I went out and bought some sand and a lot of stuff called cement fondue, and then I made a metal armature to build the thing on to, and . . . oh, it was so heavenly. I worked and worked and I didn't bother to eat much and when I was tired I just collapsed on the camp bed and slept until I woke up. I don't suppose I'll ever have such a wonderful time again as long as I live.'

'In that case, why did you come back?'

'Awful as you all are, I missed you. In the end it got so bad it was like toothache.'

'Thank you,' Val said formally. Then added: 'But what about Father and Mrs Forrest?'

'What about them?'

'Aren't they going to get married or something?'

'Good God, Val, you'll end up running a matrimonial bureau! No – Mary came round here because

129

although she saw my point about wanting to get away so that I could work in peace, she thought that someone ought to keep an eye on you all. So I said that she could, provided she promised not to spill the beans. And she obviously didn't, bless her.'

'But why didn't you tell us what you were doing in the first place? And why didn't you want us to know where you'd gone?'

'I didn't explain because I knew you'd have persuaded me not to go at all, and I'd have compromised, and kept on trying to fit in my sculpture when I had time for it after everything else. And if I'd told you where I'd gone, you'd all have come running after me – particularly Father. And speaking of Father, where is he?'

'I don't know. Probably gone out and found himself a little room where he can do things in peace –'

'I suppose I asked for that,' Mud said with a rueful grin. 'Are the twins with him?'

'I don't know that, either. We've all got pretty good at doing our own thing since you left.'

'Val,' Mud got up from her chair. She looked thin and tired, Val thought. 'Val, you still think I've been having a thingummy with Bill Bridge, don't you? You don't believe I've been working.'

Val stood up too. 'It's not a question of whether I believe you or not, because I just don't care any more. What you do is nothing to do with me, because I'm going to leave home, too. Only I'm going for good, like Theo, and I'm –'

She wanted to say a lot more. A lot more crushing,

wounding things, but it seemed as if Mud wasn't listening because all she said was: 'Where's the wheelbarrow?'

'In the garden hut, I suppose.'

'Fetch it,' Mud said. 'And wheel it round to the front of the house.'

'Why?' Val's lower lip jutted mutinously.

'Never mind. Just do as I say.'

Mud disappeared towards the hall, and against her better judgement Val slouched out to the garden hut. The wheelbarrow was a huge old wooden one inherited from Grandfather Hope, and she trundled it slowly along the darkening alleyway with Sheepshanks following behind, still trailing his rope.

Mud was standing by her old Mini traveller. 'Wheel it round to the back,' she said, and began to unlock the doors.

Val did so, and beheld a large object shrouded in a sheet.

'It's too heavy to carry, so we'll have to trundle it,' Mud said.

'What is it?'

'Never mind. Wait and see.'

It took a long while to inch the large object towards the doors, and then to manhandle it into the wheelbarrow. The grey summer darkness made everything look mysterious and rather sinister.

'Easy does it . . .' panted Mud. 'Now, you push the barrow while I hold it steady. If it slips, all is lost.'

'But what *is* it?'

Mud didn't reply, and apart from telling Sheep-shanks to get out of the way, remained silent all the time they trundled back along the alleyway.

They went in through the gate, up the path and, on Mud's instructions, straight into the kitchen.

'Now,' said Mud. 'Out of the barrow and on to the floor.'

The object was incredibly heavy, but at last they managed to heave it out. It stood between the wheel-barrow and the table, a large, ghostly-looking lump beneath its crumpled sheet. Sheepshanks began to bark at it.

'Right,' said Mud, standing back. 'Now you can look.'

'You mean take the cover off?'

'Yes, of course. Shut up, Sheepshanks –'

Very hesitantly Val twitched at the sheet. It half fell off. She gave another twitch and the sheet fell round the base of the object like a gracefully fallen skirt.

'Oh. Oh, goodness . . .'

'D'you like it?'

Val didn't say anything; just gave a long sort of sigh.

It was the figure of a girl made out of a dark grey substance. She was sitting with her knees drawn up under her chin, her arms linked round her shins, and her hair was half curly, half untidy, and her strong beautiful features were full of a wistful, thoughtful, dreaming intelligence. It was half-lifesize and amazingly real.

'It's you,' Mud said.

'Me?'

'Yes. And I don't suppose I'll ever be able to do anything so good ever again.'

'You mean it's really me? That I really look like that?'

'Yes,' Mud said. 'In a funny, daft sort of way you're absolutely beautiful. And all the time I was away I couldn't help thinking about you – *seeing* you. And so, there you are.'

'You mean – you missed me too?'

'I missed you something rotten,' Mud said. 'And now let's shut up or we'll both start crying.'

So they pulled themselves together. Mud crumpled up the sheet and threw it into a corner while Val hurried to put the kettle on for a cup of something or other, and then very quietly and unobtrusively Father came in, one twin lying motionless over his shoulder like a sack and the other one drooping at his side.

'Penny,' he said. 'Your car's outside.'

'Yes, I know,' Mud said, with a lopsided grin. 'And I've come inside. If you don't mind, that is.'

'Feel free,' Father said, and deposited the sleeping twin into the nearest container. Which happened to be the wheelbarrow. The other twin stumbled across to Mud and sleepily, lovingly, embraced her knees.

She sat down with it in a chair, and it curled up in her lap and fell instantly asleep. It looked like Bardo, but no one could be sure. At that particular point, no one could be sure of anything.

'Where on earth have you been, Paul?' Mud asked, glancing up at the clock.

'I could ask you the same thing.'

'I've been working. And look what I made.'

'With the help of Bill Bridge?'

'Once and for all, Bill Bridge had nothing whatsoever to do with it. And while we're on the subject, I have not, repeat not, been having an affair with Bill Bridge any more than you've been having one with dear old Mary Forrest.'

'How do you know I haven't?' Father demanded, and listening avidly, Val caught her breath.

Mud laughed merrily. 'Because I know she wouldn't be interested – any more than the dashing Bill Bridge would be interested in me. Let's face it, darling, at our time of life and with all our faults, only us would love each other.'

Wincing at her grammar and smiling at the sight of her sitting in the chair cuddling Bardo, Father said: 'I could still do with a little more in the way of explanation, if you could bear with me. Like, where have you been, and why did you go, and have you come back for good –'

'I'll answer the last one first,' Mud said, 'and the others can wait. It's yes.'

'Yes, you've come back for good?'

'Yes.'

'Good,' said Father, and Val thought well, if I had his famous command of the English language I'd have said something a bit more thrilling than that.

Aloud she said: 'But, Father, you still haven't said where *you've* been.'

'We went to the pictures,' he said. 'It was a thing called *Ghouls from the Galaxy* – a bit far-fetched, I thought, but the boys loved it . . . Are we going to have some coffee or something?'

'I'm making it,' Val said.

And then while Father went round to look at Mud's truly incredible new Work of Art, there was a ring at the front doorbell and Val nearly dropped a bottle of milk when she turned round from the fridge.

'*Alice!*'

'Yes, I know,' said Alice. 'But I had to come over before we went on holiday because I've been so worried about you –'

'Worried? You? Why?' Val stood with the milk bottle upraised.

'I don't really know. But you've been so funny lately that I couldn't help wondering if there was something wrong with – with . . .'

Her spectacled eyes looked round the Hopes' kitchen. At Mrs Hope and Bardo in the chair, at Bertie lying asleep in a wheelbarrow (a *wheelbarrow*?), at Mr Hope on his hands and knees examining a big dark grey statue, at Sheepshanks attached to a long length of rope as he lay chewing someone's slipper . . . and she knew that there couldn't be anything wrong. This was exactly how the Hopes always were.

'I expect it was just exam nerves that made you seem funny,' she said finally.

'Yes, I expect so,' Val agreed. 'Want some coffee?'

She turned round, then stopped abruptly: 'Hey,

Alice, what are you doing out on your own after dark? I thought –'

Alice smirked, and Val's astonishment increased when she noticed for the first time that she was wearing a trace of eyeshadow and a touch of lipstick.

'I've decided that it's time to strike out on my own,' Alice said. 'Mummy and Daddy still think of me as a little girl, and they've just got to face the fact that I'm not any more. So I told them that I was going to see a friend and that I wouldn't be home before ten-thirty.'

'Oh, Alice . . .' Val said helplessly.

'Well, we all have to start some time, don't we?' Alice said. 'Striking out, I mean.'

Looking across the kitchen she saw that Mr and Mrs Hope were holding hands and gazing into each other's eyes. No doubt about it, the whole family was funny, not just Val.

All the same, she couldn't help liking them.

But that wasn't the end of it – not by a long chalk. Suddenly, as if to make up for the emptiness in the house over the past weeks, people started arriving thick and fast. Alice and the Hopes were sitting round the table drinking coffee and eating tomato sandwiches when there was a tap on the kitchen door and Mrs Forrest appeared.

'I popped round to return the latchkey,' she said, 'because I don't think I'll be needing it any more. And incidentally, I met this young man lurking outside the garden gate.'

'Lurking with intent?' demanded Father.

'Shouldn't be surprised.'

They all sat staring at him with varying degrees of suspicion. Blue jeans, faded anorak, rumpled bob of brown hair and a large piece of sticking plaster above his right eye.

'Rob!' Val and Alice said simultaneously.

'Excuse me,' Rob said, looking rather nervous, 'but I called round because I was worried about Val. She's seemed so – well, different – these last few weeks, and I also came because –'

'Yes?' Mud and Father said together.

Rob squared his shoulders, cleared his throat and stared across at them with a hint of defiance. 'I came because I wanted you to know that she – Val, that is – saved my life this afternoon. We went swimming, well, I persuaded her to come, and I dived in off a fountain-thing and hit my head and if it hadn't been for Val I'd have drowned. And I thought I'd come and tell you because being the sort of girl she is I was pretty sure she wouldn't tell you herself.'

For a moment no one said anything. Then they all started talking at once, asking questions and exclaiming in surprise that Val could be so brave (and so *sensible*, someone said), and Val went crimson with embarrassment and hurriedly began making some more coffee.

The sound of their voices woke up the twin who was in the wheelbarrow. He gave a high shriek, and pointed to the uncurtained window by the back door.

'It's the Chief Ghoul! Look out there – it's the Chief Ghoul of the Galaxy!'

Everyone stopped in mid-word and looked to where he pointed. And at the face that was looking in.

'My heavens,' breathed Mrs Forrest. 'What on earth is it?'

A pale rounded face like a cheese, topped by a silky green coxcomb of hair. Two round dark eyes like holes burnt in a blanket and a nose squashed to a white blob against the glass.

'*The Chief Ghoul – it's him!*'

'No, it's not,' cried Mud, hastily dumping Bardo on to Father. 'It's *Theo!*'

She came in hesitantly, like some kind of nervous stray animal, and it was Alice – Alice of the impeccable manners taught by Mummy and Daddy – who went across to her with outstretched hand.

'Hello,' she said. 'How do you do? I'm Alice, and I called round to see Val. She's my best friend.'

'Great,' Theo said. She shook Alice's hand briefly, then dropped it as if she were unused to human contact. 'Any coffee going?'

'You *are* really one of the Ghouls, aren't you?' Bertie said, staring up at her anxiously. 'I mean, you don't sound like them, but –'

'It's one of the women ones,' Bardo said, who had also woken up. 'They always have a few women ones around to do the washing up.'

'You see?' Mud said to Mrs Forrest. 'You see what I'm up against?'

'I see,' Mrs Forrest laughed. 'But you can't go back to Lilian's attic now, Penny, dear, because she's about to let it to another friend, who wants to store trunks in it.'

Over by the stove Val was saying to Rob: 'I can't get over you coming all this way just to say what you said. I mean, I didn't really save your life.'

'Yes, you did,' Rob said. 'But I felt too groggy at the time to realize it.'

'How's your poor old head now?'

'Fine,' said Rob. 'I've got three stitches in it.'

'Oh, Rob . . .'

'Oh, Val . . .'

She did like him very much, after all. And it was pretty obvious that he liked her, too.

'I feel like I been dangling in space, man,' Theo was saying to Father, sitting close to him at the table.

'Your brothers evidently go along with that.' He took her hand and patted it. 'Feel like coming home now, Theo?'

'You mean grow my hair and wear shoes and all that jazz?'

'My dearest girl, I don't care whether your scalp sprouts Axminster carpet, whether you go about in bedsocks or bother boots –'

'Bovver –'

'It's entirely up to you. But the family's drawing together again, and you're part of it –'

'Careful, man,' Theo said. 'I don't exactly dig the claustrophobia bit . . .'

But what Father said was true. They were all drawing together again, and in the process they were drawing in Alice and Rob and Mrs Forrest, and although only a fool would call it A Happy Ending, or go on about They All Lived Happily Ever After – Val knew that from now on things were going to be different; happier, nicer, better.

'*Oh, super-silly us!*' she cried, hastily making some more tomato sandwiches.

'Who's supercilious?' asked Alice. (Trust her.)

*Some other Puffins*

## MAURA'S ANGEL
### *Lynne Reid Banks*

Set in contemporary Belfast, this is a moving story of everyday
courage in the face of violence, with a saving touch of magic.

## THE COMPUTER NUT
### *Betsy Byars*

When Kate receives a message on her computer from a mysterious admirer, she hopes it's her secret crush, Willie Lomax. But
she eventually discovers – no thanks to 'help' from her best
friend Linda – that Willie is not the culprit. In fact, Willie turns
out to be a resourceful computer sleuth when the two team up
for hilarious close encounters with the alien comedian.

## DRAGON DANCE
### *John Christopher*

The third story in the *Fireball* trilogy. It completes the story of
Brad and Simon who were transferred into an alternative para-
llel world by a Fireball. In this novel they go to China. (The
previous titles are *Fireball* and *The Guardians*.)

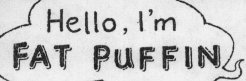